THE LOKI WOLF

THE LOKI WOLF

Arthur G. Slade

To S.T. Michael's,

Best Wishes!

Art Slade

ORCA BOOK PUBLISHERS

Canadian Cataloguing in Publication Data
Slade, Arthur, G. (Arthur Gregory)
The Loki wolf

(Northern frights)
ISBN 1-55143-145-9

I. Title. II. Series: Northern frights (Victoria, B.C.)
PS8587.L343L64 2000 jC813'.54 C00-910195-0
PZ7.S628835Lo 2000

Library of Congress Catalog Card Number: 00-100929

Orca Book Publishers gratefully acknowledges the support of our publishing programs provided by the following agencies: the Department of Canadian Heritage, The Canada Council for the Arts, and the British Columbia Arts Council.

Cover design by Christine Toller
Cover painting by Ljuba Levstek
Printed and bound in Canada

IN CANADA:
Orca Book Publishers
PO Box 5626, Station B
Victoria, BC Canada
V8R 6S4

IN THE UNITED STATES:
Orca Book Publishers
PO Box 468
Custer, WA USA
98240-0468

02 01 00 • 5 4 3 2 1

This novel is dedicated to my brothers David, Ken, and Brett, who have all supported me in their own ways. And no, none of the characters are based on any of them.

And I'd also like to dedicate this novel to all the Icelanders out there. Thanks for letting me borrow bits and pieces of your wonderful stories and heritage. I may have inadvertently changed the schedule for the Nordurleid bus to Hvammstangi and the Icelandair flight from New York to Keflavík. They will be running at the proper time from this moment forward.

I would like to thank my wife, Brenda Baker, for her editing skills and my publisher, Bob Tyrrell, for the same. I also want to give a special tip o' the Viking helmet to Jón Jónson for reading a rough draft of this novel and to Brynjólfur Gíslason, who was kind enough to tell me a little about his home town of Hvammstangi. And I perhaps owe the most to Snorri Sturluson (1179-1241), who was an Icelandic historian, poet, and chieftain best known for his Prose Edda, a prose account of the Norse myths. Without his version of the myths, these books wouldn't have been possible.

» 1 «

One week before my trip to Iceland, I died in my sleep.

Not a real death, of course. Very few healthy, fifteen-year-old girls pass away in their beds. No, I died inside one of my own nightmares. In the dream I fell from a great height — a cliff or a tower — and every bone in my body shattered when I landed on a pile of pointed stones. I awoke immediately, lying in a chilling pool of my own sweat. I didn't sleep again for hours.

The next night I drowned in a wild ocean, the undertow pulling me down until water filled my lungs. Or was it the undertow? Did something — a giant sea serpent perhaps — have a grip on me? The last thing I saw before waking was the surface getting farther and farther away.

On the third night the worst nightmare — the very worst — invaded my mind. I was running barefoot through a deserted town in a strange country, the Northern Lights drifting through the sky. Soon the town disappeared and I sprinted across a rocky plateau, gasping for breath, my long, red hair flowing in the air. Loping behind me was a gigantic wolf, its jaws snapping together and tearing off pieces of my flesh. There was no blood. No pain. But bit by bit he swallowed chunks of my body until nothing of Angela Laxness remained.

I awakened, sweating and cold. I had somehow knocked over my night table, breaking my lamp. The noise was enough to bring my mother to my bedside. I couldn't explain to her what had frightened me. In fact I could barely speak; I was too busy trying to catch my breath. She held me like she used to when I was a kid, whispering, "It's going to be all right, Angie. It's just a nightmare. You're safe. You're safe."

I dreamed of the giant wolf the next three nights in a row. My parents believed these nightmares were happening because I was worried about my upcoming trip to Iceland. Though I've traveled to Canada and to a few of the states near our acreage in North Dakota, I've never been across the ocean. "It's just your subconscious working through the new experience," my father said. "It's nothing to be ashamed of. You'll be safe. You'll be with your grandfather and your cousins. You'll get to see the farm our family came from."

I nodded and said, "Yes, you're right. I'll be safe."

My parents weren't going along because this trip was Grandpa's Christmas gift to the grandchildren and he wanted to show us the sights on his own. I'm sure Mom and Dad had considered calling the whole thing off in the last few days. I didn't know if I'd be that upset about missing it.

You see, I'd had nightmares like this a few weeks after my younger brother Andrew died in a car accident. He was traveling with our neighbors to a hockey game and they were rear-ended by a large truck. It was a miracle anyone survived. Our neighbors did. My brother didn't.

It all happened five years ago, when I was ten. I had a recurring nightmare where the sides of a car were closing in on me until I couldn't breathe. Nothing anyone said or did could make the nightmares go away. Then one night Andrew appeared in my room, looking the same as he had in life, medium-length blonde hair, a warm smile. Except he was ... ethereal. I think that's the right word. He touched my shoulder and whispered, *"Just let it go, Angie. There was nothing you could do. Let it all go."* Then he was gone. I haven't had a nightmare since.

Until the wolf came loping into my dreams.

My parents told my grandfather all about this phantom wolf. Grandpa Thursten is my mother's father and he's Icelandic to the core. He lives in Canada just outside Gimli, Manitoba, the site of the largest Icelandic settlement in North America. He knows every story about ghosts, dreams, Norse gods, and wolves.

The night before we were supposed to leave on our trip, Grandpa phoned and quietly grilled me with questions: *Do you remember the very start of the dream? Describe the wolf. Was it gray? Why were you barefoot? Were there stars or a moon in the sky?* I answered everything with as much detail as I could. Then he was quiet.

"What are they about, Afi?" I said into the receiver. *Afi* is Icelandic for Grandfather. We grandchildren rarely use it — only when we want to let him know that we're serious.

"You'll be all right," he said, "I promise. You will be all right."

» 2 «

I am telling this in the wrong order.

I should have started out by saying who my ancestors were and who I am. That's how all the Icelandic sagas begin — I know this because I've read most of the ones in my mom's collection. And all the Norse myths too. They always start with "so and so" was related to "so and so" and then "so and so" got in a boat and killed "so and so." And they end by telling you who "so and so's" offspring was. In Iceland it's important to know who you're related to.

That must be why Mom spends her spare time researching our family tree. She and Dad are constantly trying to find out more about who we're descended from, what deeds defined their lives, what land they lived on, and how all of this made us into who we are today.

They even know which bones belong to which side of the family. "Our past is written all across your face, Angie,"

Mom has often explained. "Your green eyes come from your father's side, your thin cheekbones are just like your grandma's, you can thank your Grandpa Thursten for making you so thin —"

"— and your red hair is a freak of nature," Dad would always interject. They never did explain why I ended up being left-handed, even though they were both righties.

Then they would tell me stories about the "so and so's" we're descended from. Inevitably the lecture would end up with a story about Grettir Asmundson, a hero who lived in Iceland many years ago. He was known for being big and mean and for beating up on a few ghosts and undead monsters. He was also an outlaw, but Mom and Dad usually glossed over that part.

Whenever my parents were done their lesson in genetics, Mom would sum it all up with: "If you don't know your own past, you can't know who you are."

So I will begin by saying, I am Angela Laxness, the daughter of Deidre and Jón Laxness of North Dakota. Through my mother's side of the family, the Asmundson's, I can trace our ancestry back to Grettir the Strong, a famous hero.

It's a big deal in Iceland.

» 3 «

The worst place to put someone with a fear of heights is a window seat in a jet that's about to climb 30,000 feet above the Atlantic Ocean. Yet that's the seat Grandpa Thursten gave me. "It's better to face your fears," he whispered, his lips curling into a knowing smile.

Easy for him to say. He fell asleep before we'd even left the tarmac at New York. He missed me digging my fingers into the armrests until I broke one of my nails. It would take a couple weeks to grow it back to the right length. I held my breath as the weight of the Boeing's momentum crushed against my chest and we took to the air.

A hand gently touched my shoulder and I tensed up.

"Take a deep breath," my cousin Sarah whispered from behind me. Grandpa's seat was back and Sarah was able to squeeze her hand through the open space. I'd admitted to her earlier that I wasn't looking forward to hurtling through the sky at hundreds of miles an hour. "Breathe in, then out. Everything will feel a lot better once you've got some air in your lungs."

I heard Michael, Sarah's twin brother, chuckle, and I felt a sudden anger. He was always being the smart alec. I turned to tell him to shut up, but the jet engines' kicked into overdrive, forcing me against the seat.

I eventually did take a breath. And another. And another. Until I thought I'd hyperventilate. I'd braided my hair because my mom said it would be easier to travel without it flapping all over the place — I was sure the braids had loosened and individual hairs were sticking up like porcupine quills. So much for looking sharp on my first trip to Iceland.

After several hours of flying I actually began to get comfortable, staring out the jet's window into the early morning darkness, trying to spot land. We'd been served a meager breakfast of bagels and slightly warm scrambled eggs. I was surprised my stomach wasn't upset. I had control of my breathing, my heartbeat had slowed, and I'd unclamped my hands. Maybe Grandpa was right; it *was* better to face your fears. At least I could look out at the wing and see that it was still attached.

"Have you had any more skull guests?" Grandfather asked.

Two seconds ago he was asleep in his seat, snoring softly. Now he was wide awake, his deep blue eyes staring into mine. He had a rather big, slightly crooked nose and he looked like each lesson he'd learned in his lifetime had given him a wrinkle — and there were lots of wrinkles. His thick white hair was styled like Einstein's.

"Skull guests?"

"Dreams, I mean. They used to be called skull guests in the sagas, because they came and stayed — like bad guests. Did any more of them drop by?"

"No. Not since we talked on the phone. I don't remember having any dreams at all last night." And it was true. The big, bad wolf had left me alone, off loping through someone else's nightmare, I'd supposed, looking for another Little Red-headed Riding Hood.

"Good. Perhaps they meant nothing, then."

Perhaps? What did that mean?

"They did get me thinking, though," Grandpa continued, "about Thorgeir Tree-Foot."

"Who?" Michael asked. Grandpa's seat was leaning far enough back that Michael and Sarah were able to peek at us, their blue eyes glittering, white-toothed grins splitting their thin faces. We were the same age, they were my best friends, and we had a lot in common, but I have to admit there was something a little odd about them. First, it kind of freaked me out how similar they were — dark hair, pale skin, with their heads absolutely crammed full of old Norse myths and legends. They weren't identical twins, but every time I saw them they appeared more and more alike.

Despite that, I was happy to spend some quality time with them. They lived in Missouri and we hadn't had much of a chance to talk in the last year or so.

Grandpa narrowed his bushy eyebrows. "So none of your parents has ever mentioned my dad, Thorgeir Tree-Foot?"

"Our great-grandfather was called Tree-Foot?" Michael asked, that typical smart-aleck tone in his voice. "So that's why I'm always tripping over my own feet."

"That's from not being able to chew gum and walk at the same time," Grandpa Thursten quipped. He waited for a comeback, received none, so he carried on. "Do you know how he got that name?"

This was starting to sound familiar to me. Mom had told me this story when I was younger, but I couldn't remember any of the details. "No," I admitted.

"Your great-granddad had dreams just like yours, Angie. Potent dreams. Every night for a fortnight he dreamed he was going to lose his leg. It would get caught in a trap. Or he'd be building a fence and his axe would slip and sever his leg below the knee. Or, and he always said this was the most terrifying dream, a great serpent came from beneath the water and bit it off, leaving him in the middle of the ocean, trying to swim home with only one leg. The outcome of the nightmares was always the same: he would awake covered with sweat and reach down to be sure his leg was still there."

I shuddered. The passengers across the aisle — an old guy in a brown beret and his middle-aged wife — were glancing our way now, which inspired Grandpa to raise his voice even louder. He'd use the intercom if the stewardess would let him.

"One day my father had to take a trip from Bjarg to Hof, twenty miles or so across some of the most treacherous ravines in north-central Iceland. It's not far from Thordy's farm, where we'll be staying." Thordy was one of Grandpa's nephews. I recalled Mom and Dad telling me some sad story about his wife dying, but I'd have to ask Grandpa about it later. He was too deep into this story already. "Make no mistake, the homeland is a place of beauty *and* death. One moment you'll be admiring a breathtaking waterfall; the next you'll be at the bottom of a cliff, watching the ravens descend to pick your bones. Your great-granddad was only nineteen at the time, unmarried, and searching for summer work. He'd heard that a sheep farmer was looking for help, so he hiked through the mountains, whispering the ancient rhymes his father had taught him, lines to ward away the specters and the mischievous little Huldu Folk. He had three shiny pebbles in his pocket to leave as an offering at any cairns he passed, because he believed every ghost in Iceland desires some kind of tribute."

Grandpa was starting to really wind himself up now. He even glanced over at the couple across from us to be sure they were still listening. My heart started going a little faster in anticipation.

"But the journey was longer than my father thought it would be and it was getting close to nightfall. Soon he was alone on one of the passes, far from any crofts. All he heard was the *tick tack* of his walking stick on the path. A storm gathered overhead.

"Soft footsteps echoed off the rock walls. Then came a sound of sniffing and a low, unearthly moan that made the hairs on the back of my father's neck stand up. He quickened his pace, knowing some evil thing was behind him. He muttered all the names of the undead in hopes of dispelling his pursuer. He wasn't afraid of anyone who was alive, but he knew the ghosts of this pass and the *Uppvakníngur* — those who walk after death — were to be feared."

I was holding my breath. I let it out between clenched teeth. Ever since I was a child, Grandpa had been telling us these stories about men who walk after death and monsters thirsting for blood. Every year I thought I'd outgrown them and every year I discovered I was wrong.

"A rock fell over behind him, the breathing became louder, and he began to run across the plateau, believing he was fleeing for his very life. The paths were hard to see in the darkness and he lost his way. His pursuer growled to one side of him, so father went the opposite direction. A few minutes later he could hear someone scrambling over stones behind him. Father knew he was being herded like an animal to the slaughter. Finally the plateau narrowed and he was trapped, with a thin ledge as his only escape. He hugged close to the cliff, shuffling as quickly as he could along the path — his eyes set on freedom and safety ahead. Something was thrashing about on the plateau behind him, but he didn't dare look back.

"When he was halfway across, there was a sudden rumble above. A small boulder hit him, then another, and finally a hail of rocks and debris knocked him off the path. He rolled and tumbled down, end over end, coming to a stop at the bottom of a ravine. A large boulder had crushed his right leg to the earth, pinning him below the knee.

"He looked around. Bleached skeletons of animals surrounded him, their bones broken in two as if a carnivore had been sucking on the marrow. Beside them were three human skulls, their brainpans cracked open.

"He heard a rustling sound followed by a heavy-throated roar. The noise came from the far end of the ravine. To his horror a black bear slouched towards him, slaver dripping from its huge jaws. He had never seen a bear before and he knew none had ever roamed Iceland. And yet here was one of the beasts. He tried to fend it off by throwing rocks but it descended without hesitation, clamping its teeth into his shoulder. Father beat at it with his hands, yelled with all his might. But it snarled and shook him back and forth, playing with him as if he were nothing more than a doll.

"It wasn't until the bear had dragged him partway out

from under the rock that he was able to grab the nearest half of his walking stick. It was thick, and the broken end was as sharp as a stake. He used all of his strength to jab it into the side of his attacker, through the thick hide and between the ribs, aiming for the heart.

"The bear screamed, a noise that sounded almost human. For the rest of his life my father heard that cry echoing in his nightmares. The bear halted and glared down at him with raging eyes. It opened its massive jaws, took a step forward, then suddenly fell over to one side and lay still. It moaned, sucked in its last breath, then slowly turned into a man, a stick embedded in his chest.

"Your great-grandfather dragged himself out from under the rock and crawled to the end of the ravine and upwards. His right leg was useless. It took all of his will to climb higher, repeating an old saying over and over in his head to keep himself going: *Cattle die, kinsmen die, I myself shall die, but there is one thing I know never dies: the reputation we leave behind at our death.* He made it to a wider trail and was discovered a few hours later by a group of traders heading for a spring market in Reykir. When they brought him back home the doctor had to remove his leg. They replaced it with a wooden stump. And that was how your great-grandfather got the name Thorgeir Tree-Foot and how his nightmares about losing his leg came true."

Grandpa settled back in his seat, a satisfied look on his face. Was this supposed to make me feel better about my own nightmares? I leaned back against my seat and tried to relax. The old man across the aisle was still gripping the armrest. I hoped Grandpa hadn't given him a heart attack.

"What did that saying mean?" I asked. "It sounded kind of morbid."

"My father had no desire to be known as the man who died alone in a chasm. He wanted people to remember him as someone who never gave up."

"What did he think attacked him?" Sarah asked. I was surprised at the serious tone of her voice.

The jet hit some turbulence, rattled for a moment. Were we in trouble? Where was the life preserver? Under the seat? I tried to remember the stewardess's emergency instructions.

Grandpa waited patiently until the shaking stopped and the plane was once again steady in the air.

"Your great-grandfather came from a different time than you or I. He believed the bear was really a shape-shifter, a son of Loki. My father had more superstitions than priests have prayers."

"What's a son of Loki?" Michael asked. "I haven't heard about them."

"Well they were these — uh — mythical creatures who could make themselves look like you or me, or shift into an animal like a bear or a —" The pilot announced that we were about to land. "It's a long story, it has to do with Loki and a giant's curse and how Iceland was created. I'll have to tell you later."

The engine slowed and the Icelandair Boeing 767 began to descend. My stomach lurched. I hoped the pilot was still in control. I looked out at a hazy, silvery-misted darkness.

Below us, glittering white and black like an uncut diamond, was Iceland. The country of my ancestors.

» 4 «

The landing was anything but smooth: the plane shuddered and hopped down the runway, tires squealing like banshees. The high-pitched metallic sound reminded me of my brother's accident — of what he would have heard in those final moments. I closed my eyes, which just made things worse. Time stretched out so it felt like an hour before we ground to a halt. My ears were ringing, my breath shallow. I unclenched one hand from the armrest and the other from Grandpa's leg.

"Thanks for letting go," he said. "I couldn't feel my toes anymore."

I was slipping into a strange state of jittery confusion. Grandpa's words echoed around me and I couldn't hear anything else. The other passengers moved in slow motion, pulling their luggage from the upper compartments, putting on their winter jackets.

I slowly sucked in some air, then let it out through my nostrils. That seemed to help. I did it again, swallowed, and my ears popped, releasing a flood of muttering and rustling sounds. People were moving at a normal speed. I stared out the window.

It was still dark. We had pulled up beside a rather odd-looking building that could have been mistaken for a large, modern church. It was called the Leifur Eiríksson Airport.

"Are you coming?" Grandpa asked. "Or you gonna take the plane home again?"

"I — I'm coming." I gathered enough of my wits to grab my handbag and get my jacket from the upper compartment. The jacket was still folded carefully and I was glad to see there weren't any wrinkles in it. I made my wobbly way towards the front of the plane, tagging along behind Michael and Sarah.

The stewardess said good-bye to us and Grandpa told her some joke in Icelandic that made her laugh and blush. He was still a charmer, even though he was older than the hills. I glanced in the cockpit and saw the co-pilot wiping sweat off his forehead. Maybe I wasn't the only one who thought it had been a rough landing.

Grandpa, done with his flirting, led us down the ramp and along the entrance tunnel. We were among the last people off the plane, so it seemed like the place was deserted.

"Did you go through a growth spurt, Michael?" I asked. He was about half a head taller than Sarah and me. "I thought we were all the same height."

Michael puffed out his chest, proud as a peacock. "It's the tall tales Grandpa's been telling — they finally had an effect on me."

"Tall tales? Is that what you think they are?" Grandpa,

who was a full head taller than Michael, reached down and messed up Michael's hair, grinning like crazy. "Why you ungrateful little ingrate. If you weren't my own flesh and blood, I'd give you —"

We stepped into the terminal. Grandpa stopped, grimaced and turned pale, dropping his shoulder bag to the floor. "Uh … uhhnn …" he moaned. He rubbed at his chest and began tottering like he was about to fall.

"What's wrong?" I asked. We gathered around, trying to keep him steady. I grabbed his hand. It was cold as a chunk of ice. Sarah and Michael held either arm. The remaining few passengers jostled by us, heading for an escalator. A young woman stopped momentarily to see if she could help, but Grandpa just waved her away. She walked on, glancing over her shoulder at us.

Grandpa's lips were set in a tight line, his face ashen. He was trying to speak. He blinked slowly.

"Afi," Sarah whispered. "Afi."

His eyes momentarily closed and I thought he would pass out, then blood came back into his cheeks and he shook his head. He knocked three times on the wood wall. "No … nothing's wrong," he whispered, hoarsely, "just … just the land spirits saying hello." He inhaled. "Iceland knows when one of its own comes home. It's been too many years. That last trip was with your grandmother, on her birthday."

"What was all the knocking for?" Michael asked.

"To get on the good side of the spirits and the Huldu Folk."

I shared a glance with Michael and Sarah. A *do-you-think-he's-going-crazy* glance.

"Don't look so worried," Grandpa said. He laughed as he regained his color. "It's an old habit, nothing more." He sucked in a few more deep breaths. A minute later he gently pushed us away. "I don't want to stand too close to you kids, your silliness might infect me." He was definitely back to his old self.

He picked up his shoulder bag, led us through customs and over to our luggage. Despite our protests he carried his own suitcase, marching straight out the front doors of the airport. I slung my backpack over one shoulder, Angie and Michael grabbed their own bags, and we struggled to keep up.

Outside, the only light came from streetlamps scattered throughout the nearly empty parking lot. Oversized snowflakes drifted like moths down to the ground, covering the waiting taxis and buses. I zipped up my jacket. Sarah did the same with her parka, which was so thick and puffy she looked like a gray marshmallow. I was glad I had thinsulate in mine. I still appeared slim but I'd stay warm. At least I hoped I would.

"What time is it?" Michael asked.

Grandpa made a big production of checking his watch. "It's about eleven in the morning. The sun should be out at noon."

"Noon!" I exclaimed. "How long does it stick around?"

"Till two in the afternoon." Grandpa held out his hand. He caught a snowflake, watched it melt in his palm. "Enjoy the sun while it's here because it won't be out at all in Hvammstangi."

"It'll be dark all the time?" Sarah asked. She and Michael had the same surprised look on their faces. They could have been mistaken for identical twins.

"Near enough to dark." Grandpa grinned, his eyes glittering. He'd obviously been waiting for this moment for a long time. "I guess I should have told you a bit more about

Iceland before bringing you here. I'm getting forgetful in my old age."

What kind of crazy holiday had I signed up for?

At least it looked like the right season. Snow glistened from the surrounding pavement and buildings. A Christmas tree, lit by multicolored lights, stood near the front of the airport.

It would be kind of weird not to have my parents around on Christmas day. And to be celebrating hours before them. Mom had given me some gift money, which I planned to spend on an Icelandic sweater. For the first time it dawned on me that they would be on their own Christmas morning. I wouldn't be waking up and walking down the stairs to see what was under the tree. Mom and Dad would be alone, with both of their children gone.

I felt my eyes water.

"The snow will melt in a day or two," Grandpa predicted. "Then it'll start to rain."

"Rain?" Michael asked. "Is this gonna be a wet Christmas?"

"It's the warm water currents that keep ol' Iceland heated up. Did I mention the wind'll probably blow most of the time too."

More good news, I thought. Was there no end to the surprises?

Grandpa waved his hand and a taxi pulled up. Soon we were heading to Reykjavík, the capital. The sky had grown brighter, though I had yet to see the familiar sun. We sped down the road, Sarah and Michael pointing when we spotted the ocean. The rocky land was a bleak and almost sinister picture, with mountains looming in the distance. "It's so barren," I whispered. "It's like winter on the moon."

"NASA used to practice moon landings in Iceland," Sarah

explained. She was sitting in the middle seat, squished between Michael and me. "It was formed by volcanoes and continental drift. Even the Ice Ages couldn't put a stop to the volcanoes."

"When did you get so smart?" Michael poked her in the ribs. "You weren't smart a few days ago. Even a few seconds ago."

Sarah held up a travel booklet, then used it as a shield against further attacks. "It's all in here."

"If we have time," Grandpa said from the front seat, "I'll take you to the largest volcano, Mount Hekla. In the Middle Ages they believed it was one of the vents of hell itself."

"Sounds like a hot place to go," I quipped.

"Please, Angie, I can only handle one smart mouth at a time," Grandpa said, pointing towards Michael. The twins laughed in unison.

We passed a few cottages and larger homes, then crossed a bridge, turned a corner, and there was Reykjavík neatly laid out before us. The city looked small and tidy, like we'd stumbled on a fairy-tale town.

We drove through the outskirts, gawking at the tall houses. Some were light blue, others gray, even red. We bumped down various narrow streets and passed a number of giant churches with tall, bell-shaped spires.

"Exactly where are we going, Gramps?" Michael asked.

"To the bus depot. Thordy will be waiting for us in Hvammstangi. I'm sure he'll be glad to have some company. He's probably been pretty lonely since his wife died."

"What did she die from?" I asked. "Mom just told me she'd passed away, but didn't say what from."

Grandpa turned to face the three of us. We leaned closer. "It's really quite sad. Two summers ago Kristjanna didn't come back from an evening walk. The home croft has some really rough land up on the plateau. When I was a kid we'd lose at least one sheep a year to the cliffs. Thordy went out looking for her and was gone for days. The family and the local constable organized a search party and scoured the area. The hired man finally discovered Thordy in a cave, far back in the mountains, with his wife cradled in his arms. She was dead and he was completely distraught, moaning and rocking her as if she was just sleeping. No one knows what killed Kristjanna. There was no sign of an aneurysm or anything like that, just one tiny wound behind her left ear."

"The poor woman," Sarah said. "And poor Thordy, too."

"Yeah," I said. "Is he doing all right now?"

"He sounded okay on the phone. But that's part of the reason why we're staying there," Grandpa explained. "To keep him company."

The cab pulled to a stop in front of a rectangular, two-story building: the bus depot. People in long coats walked around. Other younger people were wearing backpacks. No one seemed to be in much of a hurry. The sky was still dark.

Grandpa paid the driver and we began lugging our luggage to the depot. I was happy I'd managed to jam all my belongings into my leather backpack. Both Sarah and Michael had their gear stuffed into two large canvas travel bags. They looked like something the military would use. Or a hockey team.

"Just wait here," Grandpa said. "I'll pick up the tickets. You can stare at the pond across the way."

» 5 «

The pond, as Grandpa had called it, was really a small lake of water across the street, guarded by a few trees. A pint-sized tower sat on one bank. Buildings were reflected in the waves in the dim light. I wondered how this land would have looked when our ancestors first arrived on their Viking boats. Somehow they had built a city from nothing, making a place of safety and warmth.

A four-passenger plane buzzed above the water and over us, so near we ducked. "The airport's right there," Michael said, pointing at a landing strip behind the bus depot. "Man, they sure pack everything close together."

A minute later Grandpa came out with a handful of tickets and led us to a red bus with white lines across its side. The name *Nordurleid* was on the front. It was about half the size of a normal bus. I set my backpack on top of the other luggage and lined up behind Michael and Sarah.

The driver was a long-armed man with a beard as thick as unraveled wool. He greeted us with two gruff words: "*Gódan dag.*" We all said *hello* back to him. He took our tickets, motioned to the bus and began throwing our luggage in the storage compartment.

Inside, there were only about five other riders, though at least fifty seats. "Better settle in," Grandpa said, "it's a long way to Hvammstangi." He paused, gave us a sly smile. "Hey, that could be a song." He began to sing to the tune of "It's a Long Way to Tipperary." "*It's a long, long way to Hvammstangi, but my heart's right there.*" Grandpa bowed, then sat next to a window.

We started on our way. The wind whistled through the spaces between the sliding windows, cold drafts of air ran across my bare neck like ghostly fingers. I pulled on the window, but it was shut as far as it could go. I huddled in my jacket, hugging myself.

About ten minutes later it dawned on me how quiet we all were — which wasn't that strange for Sarah, but Michael's mouth usually ran at 200 rpm's. I glanced over at him. He was staring ahead, his eyes glazed over. "You on another planet, Michael?" I asked.

"No, I'm —"

"Dreaming of Fiona," Sarah interjected.

"Shut your —" Michael began.

"What?" I cut him off. "You're still writing to her? This must be serious. Is she your true love? Your one and only? Your reason for —"

"Please, stop this soap opera!" Grandpa shook his head. "This trip will be long enough without hearing about the heart-wrenching agony of teen romance. We're about ten hours away from Hvammstangi."

"What!" Michael exclaimed.

"I'm kidding. Couple more hours should do it." Grandpa pointed out the window. "The coast is that way. In fact we're not far from an outcropping that's sometimes called Skrymir's nose."

"Is Angie's side of the family descended from Skrymir?" Michael asked. "Is that why her nose is so big?"

"My nose isn't big!" I shouted. And it wasn't. It was petite. Maybe even too small, the Laxness nose I'd inherited from my father. "It's nowhere near the size of the Asmundson nose."

"Please, you two, stop squabbling!" Grandpa shook his head, feigning shame. "Just use those big ears you all inherited from me for listening. I'll tell you who the sons of Loki are. It has to do with how Iceland was created, not by these so-called continental drifts, but by one of the gods." He cleared his throat, a universal sign that he was about to start one of his stories. "You see, one day Loki, the trickster god, dared Thor to battle with the largest of the giants, Skrymir. He was a hundred times taller than Thor, his very shoulders held up the sky. Thor tracked him down, which wasn't hard considering the size of his tracks. He challenged Skrymir to a fight, then began swinging his mighty hammer, Mjollnir, again and again at the giant. The battle raged across all nine worlds, over mountains and lakes and valleys. Villages were crushed by the giant's feet, fissures torn in the ground by Thor's hammer. Through it all Skrymir laughed, saying, *'Shoo shoo pesky red-haired fly.'*

"Loki hatched a plan to help Thor defeat the giant. The trickster god slyly asked Skrymir to prove his strength by catching a hundred whales. Skrymir waded into the ocean. Thor jumped aboard a boat and paddled after him. While Skrymir was under the water searching for whales, only his head was exposed above the waves. Thor leapt atop him, hammering at his skull. Wherever he struck, rocks and flame spewed forth. Then ice and snow. Rocks and flame, ice and snow. Finally Thor gave the giant such a powerful blow in the center of his skull that Skrymir's entire body turned to stone.

"Skrymir's final words before his lips froze in place forever were a curse on Loki, telling him that his children would be forced to live on this new island as outcasts. Many ages later Loki betrayed the gods and brought about the death of Baldur, the most loved and beautiful of all the gods. The gods hunted Loki and his shape-shifting children down and turned Vali, Loki's favorite son, into a wolf. He killed his brother Narvi, whose entrails were used to bind Loki in a cave. Vali then fled, bounding away across the water to the land where the sun shines at midnight. To Iceland."

Wow. Someone getting his guts torn out. Grandpa was reaching a new height in storytelling gore. I hated to think what he'd come up with next.

Grandpa opened his mouth to say something, then closed it and rubbed his chin. "And that was that," he finished, quietly. "At least that's all I can remember."

Suddenly the lights went out. I turned, looked through the window. We were in a tunnel.

"We're just going under the fjord," Grandpa explained. "No need to get all antsy."

We eventually came out the other side, but the sky appeared much darker. Almost black.

"So is that how the myth ends?" Sarah asked. "With Vali coming to Iceland."

"Oh, no," Grandpa said slowly, "… well … myths and folktales never really end. You should know that by now.

They become part of other stories. The Irish monks were the first to land on Iceland. A few of their journals survived and they mention that they sometimes saw feral people in the shadows of the mountains. They called them *lupinus* and believed they were the spawn of the devil and that they could shift their shape into wolves or bears or whatever creature they wanted, as long as it was about the same size as they were — though most seemed to like being wolves for reasons I can't imagine. The creatures would even take the form of a familiar monk, just to lure other monks to their lair. The monks wore bells on their belts, which they rang to keep the evil ones away.

"The Vikings who came and chased off the monks spoke of the *úlfr-maðr*, the wolf men. Icelanders in the 1500s wrote about these shape-shifters building their own farms and taking human shapes to blend in."

"Where did all these stories come from?" I asked. "What are they based on?"

"Human imagination. But your great-grandfather believed they were the sons of Loki. He saw one once. In fact that's how he got his name, Thorgeir Tree-Foot. You see, it all started when he was taking a trip from Bjarg —"

"Repeat! Repeat! You told us this story on the plane," Michael said, then seeing the confused look on Grandpa's face, he softened his tone, "This morning, remember?"

Grandpa glanced back and forth between us. "I did, didn't I? Right. It seems so long ago." He drew in a breath. "Sorry, about that. I usually only tell my stories once a day." He crossed his arms and sat back. "I'll try to think up some new ones," he promised. Then, as if wanting to retreat from us, he closed his eyes.

Sarah gave me a worried look as if to say: *What's up with*

Grandpa? I shrugged my shoulders.

We traveled for some time in silence, the bus somehow managing to stay on the thin, snow-covered highway. Grandpa looked like he was asleep now. I studied his face, the wrinkles, and the white hair. He did appear older than last year. A lot older.

I shook my head. I didn't want to think about him aging. He was in his late seventies, wasn't he? That's still young for an Icelander. But when he'd had that little dizzy spell in the airport, I'd thought, briefly, that something was seriously wrong.

I glanced at my watch. It was one-thirty in the afternoon, Icelandic time, and the sky was already dark. It had been a lifetime since I'd rolled out of a New York hotel bed early in the morning to catch the flight. I needed a serious rest. I closed my eyes and slept fitfully. We stopped twice in small towns, but since Grandpa didn't move I just closed my eyes again.

The sound of the engine slowing down woke me. We had turned in to a gas station. Before I was even fully awake, we were standing outside, our luggage in our hands, watching the bus pull away.

"That's strange," Grandpa said, after surveying the area, "Thordy's supposed to be here to meet us." From where we stood, the whole town appeared empty. "I sent him a letter telling him exactly when we would arrive. Even called him a couple of days ago. We'll head downtown. It isn't far. Travels aren't over until you're safely indoors."

Which apparently meant *Let's start marching.*

» 6 «

We tramped through Hvammstangi, a small town that probably didn't have much more than seven or eight hundred residents. It appeared a little too perfect, like there were sweepers who had cleaned up the streets before our arrival, dusted the town with snow, then hid around a corner. The pavement was made of concrete flagstones, each a foot and a half wide. The houses on either side of us were one, two, or three stories tall, yet each was about the same width on the main floor. Many homes were covered with a thin metal siding that Grandpa explained was used all over Iceland.

"It looks like protection from meteorites," I said.

"Yeah," Michael agreed. He took a black headband out of his jacket pocket and slipped it over his ears. "Is it closer to space up here? We're not gonna suddenly be sucked into the atmosphere, are we?"

Grandpa made a *harrumph!* sound and tramped even

faster through the snow. We marched down what appeared to be Hvammstangi's main street. A huge Christmas tree with glittering lights stood on one side of the block. Across from it was the local tavern, a place called the *Hótel Selid*. Grandpa went through the front doors leaving us shivering outside.

"So this is northern Iceland," Michael said between clattering teeth. "It's even colder than I thought it would be."

"This is nothing," I said, shivering. "You two have been in Missouri far too long. You need a taste of a good North Dakota blizzard to remind you what cold really feels like."

"Everything seems so old here," Sarah whispered, a tone of awe in her voice. "Not just the buildings, though some of those are quite ancient, but the land. Just so much older than anything around Chillicothe."

The town was beginning to look familiar to me, like I had seen it in a photograph. But the memory was so strong it felt as though I had maybe even stood right here, exactly where I was standing.

"Are you all right, Angie?" Sarah asked.

"Yeah, your brain freeze or something?" Michael added.

I shook my head, ignoring him. I couldn't remember where I'd seen this place before. "I'm just getting my bearings, that's all."

Grandpa came out of the tavern a moment later accompanied by a middle-aged man who was wearing a sweater and walking like he didn't feel the chill. He grumbled a few words in Icelandic when he saw us. Grandpa answered, then laughed. The man remained sour.

"I can't get a hold of Thordy, so we're gonna catch a ride with my new friend, Brynjólfur," Grandpa explained. "He just wanted to make sure you didn't bite. I assured him you've all had your shots."

"Funny, Gramps," Michael said, "you're a real riot."

Brynjólfur led us to his vehicle, which was some sort of large, four-doored jeep with oversized, knobby tires. Judging by the dents and chipped paint, it had been through a couple of near death experiences. We climbed in and started bumping down the road before I could even find my seatbelt. I quickly dug around in the seat, coming up with a few pieces of garbage, and finally uncovered both ends of the belt. I didn't feel safe until I'd clicked them together and tightened it around me. The heater barely puffed out enough hot air to defrost a patch of the window directly in front of Brynjólfur. He turned out to be a worse driver than the jet pilot. Maybe they were cousins.

Minutes later we were on an icy highway, heading inland. After a few miles of jouncing around we turned and bumped down a country road into a valley. There were the occasional signs of civilization, lights of farms here and there, all made eerie through the frost-covered windows. The lights grew fewer and farther between until we were in a land of darkness lit only by our headlights. The road roughened and a dim bobbing glow came into view, grew brighter. The jeep rattled to a stop in front of a house. It was one story high, plain looking, and painted white with a beat-up, four-door, four-wheel-drive truck parked out front. No lights were on inside. Across the yard stood a smaller, older looking home that appeared to be built right into the hillside. Behind them both was the shadow of another building.

Brynjólfur didn't get out of his jeep. He waited until we had all our bags piled beside us, then mumbled a parting word to Grandpa and jammed down on the gas. The jeep's tires spun on the ice, spitting a few pieces of gravel our way.

Seconds later his taillights disappeared into the night.

"Wow!" Michael said. He stared at the sky above him.

There was no moon. The air was alive with shifting, glowing lights, brighter than the stars and so close they appeared to be skimming the top of the house. It awakened the oddest familiar feeling in me. I felt like I'd been here before, too. *Deja vu all over again.* The hairs on my arms and the back of my neck began to stand up. A cold chill crawled down my spine, a chill that didn't feel like it would go away anytime soon.

"The Northern Lights," Sarah whispered. "I've never seen them so bright. And so close."

"They're a sight for sore eyes." Grandpa craned his neck, trying to see as much of the sky as possible. "I grew up under these lights. We're definitely home." He cleared his throat. "Well, no sense getting hypnotized by the *Aurora Borealis*, not when we could be hypnotized by a blazing fire instead. Now remember, Thordy is my brother's son. So he's your … well … uncle, I guess. I hope. Or is he a cousin? Well, just call him Uncle Thordy, either way. He'll like it." Grandpa picked up his suitcase. "I don't know about you, but I'm ready for some old-time hospitality."

He strode ahead and rapped loudly on the thick door. There was a long silence. Grandpa let out a frosty, exasperated breath and pulled back his arm to give the door another good pounding, but the muffled sound of footsteps coming down a hall stopped him. They grew louder, the floor creaking like there was a huge weight moving across it. Uncle Thordy sounded like he was a giant.

The door squeaked open half an inch and a shadow stared down at us. All I could see was a glowering eye.

A gruff male voice barked something in Icelandic.

"Four weary travelers, looking for some room at the inn," Grandpa answered in English. "And some coffee!"

"Who are you?" the man asked. "Tourists? You trying to find the guest farm? Are you lost?"

"No," Grandpa laughed, "not lost. I'd recognize the croft I grew up on. It's me — Thursten Asmundson, home for the holidays."

The eye swiveled back and forth, back again. "Thursten?" the man snapped. "But he's in Canada. Not due until tomorrow."

A porch light flicked on, the high-watt bulb momentarily blinding. Grandpa bowed, a wide smile on his face.

"You're Thursten?" the man asked gruffly. "I thought you'd look different."

"I look the same as I did when I saw you ten years ago, Thordy, might have gained a wrinkle here or there."

"It — it is you. Uncle Thursten!"

The door suddenly slammed shut. I expected a warm greeting; instead we stood staring, waiting for it to open again. "I'll be right there!" Uncle Thordy exclaimed loudly, then opened and closed another door inside the house. Finally he yanked the front door open again and came out.

He was a tall, barrel-chested Icelander, his thick beard and hair speckled with gray. I'd guess he was somewhere in his late forties. His face had the familiar big-boned Asmundson look, with a long jaw and a rugged nose. He had three serious-looking scars that stretched from his right eyebrow into his hairline. He was wearing a pair of slippers, but didn't seem to mind tramping through the snow. He gave Grandpa a rib-crushing bear hug. "You've arrived early! What a surprise!"

"Surprise?" Grandpa wheezed. He coughed and Uncle

Thordy stepped back. "But we're here when we said we'd be, Thordy."

"You are?" Uncle Thordy scratched his head. "What day is it?"

"Thursday, all day," Grandpa said.

"Oh no! Oh, I'm so sorry." Uncle Thordy put one hand to his forehead like he was stricken with a sudden migraine. "I'm a day behind, I haven't been getting much sleep. I've been so confused. I was supposed to pick you up today. I'm sorry."

"It's all right. Everything worked out. It just added to the adventure of it all. The kids had fun in Thorstein's jeep."

"You survived a ride with Thorstein?" Uncle Thordy regarded the three of us. "You are tough. Look how big you three are. I've only seen pictures of you when you were tots, though I've heard quite a bit about you. The twins and Angie, our North American roots. You're all grown up!"

"Uh … hi," Sarah said. We all introduced ourselves and shook his hand. It was warm and strong. He was also wearing a layer or two of aftershave lotion. Very strong stuff.

Uncle Thordy grabbed two of the nearest bags and lugged them towards the house. "Let's talk inside." We followed him.

I was the last one through the door. I bumped it closed with my hip, set down my backpack, and was hit by a blast of heat. At least Uncle Thordy believed in using his furnace. Maybe I'd finally get the chill out of my bones. The second thing that hit me was a slightly rotten scent in the air. A smell like the garbage had been left out too long.

"Just toss your coats in the closet and throw your boots on the mat," Uncle Thordy said, opening up the closet door. "Then get your bodies into the living room."

I found a hanger and gingerly hung up my jacket. It had been expensive and I didn't want it to get creased. As I went to close the door I noticed a big axe hanging on the closet wall, large enough to take out a good-sized tree with a few whacks. Why did Uncle Thordy need such a gigantic axe? Iceland wasn't exactly the most wooded area in the world. I closed the door.

Uncle Thordy led us down the hall and past the kitchen. The smell I'd detected at the front door lingered more heavily in the air here, but the kitchen was tidy. Maybe that's why Uncle Thordy hadn't opened the door right away — he was too busy hiding the garbage. It crossed my mind that he might not be into bathing too much. Which I knew wasn't the norm here — Icelanders spent every spare moment jumping into hot springs.

Uncle Thordy guided us into the cozy warmth of his living room. Actually, it was more like a library than a living room. Two large shelves sat on either wall, stuffed with books of all sizes. I was happy to see Uncle Thordy was a reader, just like the rest of the family. I'd have to sneak a peek at his collection; maybe there were some sagas I'd never seen before. Of course, it wouldn't do me much good if they were all in Icelandic.

Next to one of the shelves was a scrawny Christmas tree, dotted with tiny versions of the Icelandic flag, a few scattered ornaments, two lines of lights, and a lopsided star that pointed at a corner of the ceiling. It looked frumpy, but it was good to see something similar to what we'd have at home. I guessed Uncle Thordy had given us his best shot at decorating.

I dropped my backpack and collapsed on a forest green couch, sitting as near to the brick fireplace as possible. A fire danced across two logs. I held out my hands, let the heat warm my fingertips.

"I'll show you where you'll be sleeping later," Uncle Thordy said, "but for now, tell me about your trip."

"It was bumpy," Michael said.

"And rough," I added. "Did we mention it was bumpy?"

"A character-building experience," Grandpa said. "Unfortunately these three weren't starting with much character." He winked at Uncle Thordy.

"We inherited all we got from you," Michael quipped.

"Well … I — I don't have a comeback. You got me that time, Michael. Guess I'm training you a little too well."

Uncle Thordy grinned at the bantering, then furrowed

his brows. "I am sorry I wasn't at the petrol station to meet you. I lost track of time. It always happens in the midwinter. There are so many hours of darkness you start to wonder when to sleep and when you should be awake. Soon your waking life becomes a long, slow dream. I am so sorry."

"You're forgiven," Grandpa said. "There's only one thing that would make up for it: a big, hot cup of …"

"Coffee! It's on its way." Uncle Thordy leapt up and went to the kitchen. The living room only had a view of the kitchen table, but not the rest of the kitchen, so I couldn't see what Uncle Thordy was up to, but with all the banging it sounded like he was conducting a symphony of pots and pans.

"Don't be too hard on ol' Thordy," Grandpa whispered. "He hasn't been the same since Kristjanna died. He even looks different, more tired, I guess. I hardly even recognized him."

A few minutes later Uncle Thordy returned with a tray full of cups and a huge metal pot of coffee. He smiled and triumphantly lifted the blue pot. It looked like something straight out of the pioneer days, covered with dents. He poured us each a cup without asking whether we wanted one. "This'll get your heart going," he promised, handing me a cup. I saw the dark bags under his eyes, the lines on his face. The scars above his right eyebrow added to the impression that he'd had a hard time lately. I knew what a heavy weight grief could be; it must have taken years off his life.

The coffee was thick as oil and steaming hot. I glanced at Sarah and Michael, who were both staring at their own cups like they'd been given poison. I'd had coffee a few times before, but this was way different. Like the long lost ancestor of coffee. I took a sip and it tasted about half as good as it looked. It was hot enough to heat my innards, though, and I was thankful for that.

"This is what Icelanders drink?" Sarah whispered. "No wonder so many of them look grumpy."

Uncle Thordy had slipped out and was back again with a plate heaped with flat, blackened pieces of bread along with strips of meat. He set it on the coffee table in front of us. "*Hangikjöt* and *flatkökur*," he announced.

"That's smoked lamb and hard bread to you," Grandpa explained.

We dug in. The bread *was* hard as cement, but I was able to bite off a big enough chunk to discover that it was fairly tasty. And the lamb melted in my mouth. I was so famished I could've eaten a ton of it. We hadn't had a bit of food since breakfast on the airplane. Uncle Thordy returned a third time with a plate of stuff called *gravlax*, which was made of salmon. It tasted salty.

"If I'd been more organized I'd have had a real meal prepared for you. Maybe even some *svid*."

"Oh, you should save that for special occasions," Grandpa said. "Plus it'd probably freak Michael out."

"Freak me out, why?"

Grandfather brushed crumbs off his shirt. "It's singed sheep's head, sawn in two, boiled and eaten fresh."

Michael turned pale, along with me and Sarah. I was the first to voice our opinion. "Ewwww!"

"We never waste anything in Iceland," Uncle Thordy began, "it's part of —"

A knock on the door cut his sentence short. He shot out of his seat, spilling coffee on his hand. "I'm not expecting company," he said, wiping the coffee on his pants. "Just wait here." He walked down the short hall and out of sight. The front door creaked open, letting a gust of wind come into the living room. It settled at our feet and chilled my legs. I slid closer to the fire.

Uncle Thordy spoke in hushed tones and another voice answered. There was a soft clunk, then the door closed.

A moment later a man followed Uncle Thordy into the room. The stranger pulled back the hood of his jacket and a few flakes of snow fell to the floor. I was surprised to see a young guy about my age, his black hair slicked back. He had a thin, fine-boned face, dark skin, and his lips were curled into a friendly smile.

"This is Mordur, my hired helper. He saw my lights were on so he came by," Uncle Thordy explained. Grandpa stood and reached out his hand. Mordur gave him an exuberant shake, saying, *"Gott kvöld."* Grandpa winced slightly, like Mordur had squeezed too tight. Mordur shook everyone else's hand, saying "Good evening" in English each time.

When he came to me, he held my hand for a few seconds longer than the others and stared at it like it was an interesting butterfly that had just landed on his palm. I was surprised how warm his hand was — burning hot. He looked me in the eyes, his were a swirling gray.

"Sugar," he said.

"Wh-what?" I muttered. I started to blush.

"Sugar. I come by for sugar." His English had a bit of an accent to it. He let go of my hand. He seemed — well — almost like he was struck with a sudden bout of shyness. "For my coffee. It makes it much … uh … more good tasting." He turned to everyone. "Welcome to Iceland! Christmas is best time to be here. The best time, I mean. It is when you get all the good food."

"Please, join us," Uncle Thordy said. "The coffee's hot."

Mordur shook his head. "No thank you. I still have to

finish dishes. Your family is here to celebrate the holiday. That is good. Have you warned them about the thirteen Santa Clauses?"

"Thirteen Santa Clauses!" I said, a little too loudly. Mordur looked my way, giving me a warm grin. His eyes strayed to the top of my head, then back. Was my hair a mess? "B-but there's just one Santa Claus, isn't there?"

"Not in Iceland. We do different things here. The thirteen Santa Clauses are the *Jólasveinar*. It means 'Christmas lads.' They are very small. Imps! I think that is the word you use. There is *Stúfur*, the itty bitty one, and *Pottasleikir* — he licks pots people leave out — *Bjúgnakrækir*, the sausage snatcher, and ten others. One comes every night for thirteen nights before Christmas and puts a gift in your shoe. Unless you are bad, of course. Then they do a bad thing. Like steal your sausages or hide your lipstick."

"Only in Iceland would they have *bad* Santa Clauses," Michael said, between bites of bread. "We're a morbid people, we are. Thirteen brats handing out presents."

"Careful," Mordur warned, shaking his finger, "the *Jólasveinar* know when you talk bad about them. You will end up with a rotten potato in your shoe."

"It's all he deserves," Sarah joked. Mordur smiled at her and I felt a sudden twinge of jealousy. She already had a boyfriend in Manitoba, why was she flirting with him?

"Tonight is the twenty-one of December, *Gluggagægir's* night. He is the window peeper. And if you are really bad, Gryla, the old hag mother of the *Jólasveinar*, will go and eat you."

"This is starting to sound more like Halloween," I said. Mordur turned towards me again. "Tricks, treats, and monsters."

Uncle Thordy set down his cup of coffee on the side table. "Don't you three listen to Mordur. He's inherited his father's long-winded, storytelling genes. And don't worry about being devoured by Gryla. The only old hag near this croft is Gunnvor and all she eats is regular food. As far as I know."

Genuine surprise showed on Grandfather's face. "You mean she's still alive? She was ancient when I was a child. I thought she would've died years ago."

Uncle Thordy rubbed his beard. "Oh, she's alive all right. Alive and kicking. I can feel her beady eyes on my back every time I head out to the pasture. She puts the spook in the horses, too."

"Then she hasn't changed." Grandpa Thursten shook his head in disbelief. "She used to come down to where we played by the marsh and threaten to break our bones and throw us in a cairn if we kept making a racket."

"She may be Gryla in disguise," Mordur said, laughing. "Anyway, I do need sugar, then I will depart with all your wonderful guests." He slapped his forehead. "I mean leave you with all your guests. Sorry, my English is rusted. It has been months since I used it." He shrugged.

"It's okay," I said, "your English is a thousand times better than my Icelandic." I smiled, then wondered if I had salmon stuck in my teeth. My cheeks flashed with heat. For the millionth time I cursed my pale white complexion. I was probably as red as the nose on Rudolph the Red-Nosed Reindeer. Mordur glanced at the top of my head again and I resisted the urge to pat down my hair. Sarah caught my eye and winked.

Mordur followed Uncle Thordy into the kitchen and came out with a small paper bag of sugar.

"It was good meeting you all," Mordur said, then left. A moment later the door down the hall opened and banged shut.

"He's young for a hired man," Grandpa remarked.

Uncle Thordy nodded. "He is. Just sixteen. He's the son of my previous hired man, Einar. Einar drowned last summer while fishing at sea. A terrible, tragic accident. He left Mordur with nothing but a few month's savings and the clothes on his back. His mother lives in France and didn't want anything to do with him."

"How'd he learn English?" Sarah asked.

"Mordur isn't much for school, but he's smart as a whip. He picked up his English from tourists and other Icelanders. We all know pieces and bits of two or three different languages. He's good at most everything he wants to be good at and the animals do what he says, so I decided to keep him around. Plus I felt a debt to his father. Einar was a dependable man."

"It's always a comfort to work with someone you trust." Grandpa rubbed at his chest as if he had some sort of sharp pain. When he saw us all watching him, he grinned. "What are you staring at? Haven't you seen an old man try to keep down a burp before?" He looked at Uncle Thordy. "Do you have any plans for us tomorrow?" he asked.

"To let you sleep as long as you want. None of the relatives arrive until tomorrow night."

Grandpa nodded. "Sleeping in sounds like a great idea. Maybe in the afternoon I can drive you kids to Bjarg. It's where Grettir the Strong grew up. We might even be able to take a trip to Drang Island, where Grettir died. Though I don't think we'd want to climb around there this time of year."

Grandpa always spoke as though it was just a couple of years ago that Grettir the Strong was alive, but in fact he lived sometime back in the 1100s, long before I set foot on this earth. According to my parents, Grettir spent most of his time fighting other Icelanders and the undead. I've always been glad our family let go of that tradition.

Grandpa reminded us we all had orders to phone home once we got to Uncle Thordy's, no matter what time it was in the States. Michael and Sarah went first and talked to their parents for a few minutes. When it was my turn my mom picked up the phone on the third ring. It was so odd to hear her voice sounding crystal clear, even though she was thousands of miles away. She and Dad were just sitting down for a late supper of hamburgers and homemade French fries. She asked me questions about the trip and I answered them all in a daze. When it came time to say good-bye, all I could say was, "I miss you."

"We miss you too, dear," Mom said.

I joined everyone in the living room and we talked for another half hour. My eyes started to burn, my lids grew heavy. It had been a long, trying trip and jet lag seemed to have caught up with me. Uncle Thordy saw one of my yawns. "It doesn't matter what country you're in," he said, "a yawn means the same thing. I'll show you to your rooms."

We grabbed our luggage and Uncle Thordy led us down a short hall, the walls white and bare. Sarah and I would share a room. Michael had to settle for a cot in Uncle Thordy's tiny office. Grandpa took a room down the hall from us. We said good night to Uncle Thordy and Michael.

"I'm glad to have you girls along," Grandpa said quietly to us. "I do feel lucky to have grandchildren like you two. And Michael, of course."

"Have a good sleep, Afi," Sarah said.

As he turned away I noticed a dark spot on the back of his shirt. "Grandpa, what's that?"

He turned to me, then looked over his shoulder at where I was pointing. It was a red stain.

"Did you cut yourself?" Sarah asked.

"Not that I know of," Grandpa answered. "I'll check it out in the mirror. Guess I must have leaned on something sharp. Good night." He closed the door.

Once we were in our room I dropped my backpack next to a cot. I went to the washroom and decided to have a quick bath. The water here got hot *real* fast. Maybe it came directly from a hot spring. My hair actually looked okay. I'm not sure why Mordur kept staring at it. A few minutes later I was clean and perfectly toasty.

» 8 «

"How are you feeling now, Angie?" Sarah was sitting up in her bed, reading a thick paperback novel. "I know you're not much into airplanes." Her brown hair was undone so it fell across one shoulder. She'd let it grow since the last time I'd seen her and it made her look more sophisticated.

"I'm better," I admitted, towel drying my hair. It was down to my shoulders. It'd be awhile before it would catch up to Sarah's. "Once we landed I calmed down. Of course the bus ride didn't help much. Or the car ride."

"It hasn't exactly been an uneventful trip so far, has it?"

"It was a little weird how Uncle Thordy forgot to pick us up." I grabbed my brush and began working on the tangles in my hair. "And then he wasn't all that friendly until he found out who we were."

"Maybe they're more paranoid here than we are at home. Or more superstitious. But I got the same vibes. He was relieved to see it was us."

"Do you find the house a little stinky?" I asked.

Sarah nodded. "I don't think Uncle Thordy's all that careful about keeping everything clean. Plus I think he's a little depressed. I get the feeling if we lifted the rugs we'd find a lot of dust bunnies."

Done with my hair, I dropped my brush on the night table and tucked myself under the biggest, thickest comforter I'd ever seen. We were quiet for a few moments. There were tons of things I wanted to ask Sarah, about her boyfriend, how her mom and dad were, what was new in her life, but I just couldn't find the energy.

But somewhere beneath all my tiredness, my heart was beating double-time. The coffee had kicked it into high gear. The last thing I needed was to be tossing and turning all night.

"Don't take this the wrong way," Sarah said, measuring each word, "but you don't seem as, well — up — as you usually are. I always think of you as being Suzy Sunshine, but you're not quite like that right now. Is everything all right? Or is it just the long trip?"

Sarah had a gift for being able to sense my deeper moods better than anyone, even my parents. "I — I've been thinking about my brother a lot lately. The closer I got to this holiday, the more I thought about him."

"It's been five years, hasn't it?"

"Yes. A long time. But the older I get, the more I miss him. Or the more I understand what it means to not have him around anymore."

"I miss him too, Angie. Andrew was a great kid. As much as Michael gets on my nerves, I can't imagine what it would be like if he was gone."

We fell silent. What else was there to say? He was gone and we missed him.

But there *was* something else. I opened my mouth to tell Sarah about the nightmares I'd had back at home, but then couldn't spit out a word. I had an overwhelming feeling that if I spoke about them, they would return. Better to leave them be.

There was one other thing bothering me, though.

"Do you think Grandpa's okay? He seems tired. More tired than I've ever seen him."

She frowned. "He *is* looking older. And he tried to tell us the same story twice in the same day. He never used to do that."

"I hope he's okay," I said.

"He probably needs rest, that's all. It was a heck of a long trip. I still can't believe we're here. Actually in Iceland. Where our family comes from." She yawned and blinked sleepily several times. "You know, I think I'll be a lot more excited about it tomorrow. How about some shut-eye?" She waited for me to nod, then clicked off the lamp. "Nighty-night."

"Good night," I whispered, my eyelids slowly shutting down. Sleep. Exactly what I needed. A chance for my brain to rest.

I hoped I was too exhausted to dream.

» 9 «

Probably the worst nightmare in all of the Old Norse myths is the one that haunted Baldur. Baldur was the purest of the gods. He was beautiful, wise, and gentle, and the son of Odin. No one wished him harm. Yet one night he had awful nightmares that made him twist and squirm in an attempt to escape the dark phantoms. He woke up, his body gleaming with sweat. He tried to remember each shape he'd seen and dispel them from his mind. But he failed. The skulking dream creatures crept away only to return again whenever he closed his eyes.

None of the gods could figure out the meaning of the dreams. Finally Odin went down to the Underworld to ask a dead seer what the dreams meant. She told him Baldur would die soon, and his death was a sign that Ragnarok — the end of the world — was coming. There was nothing any of the gods could do to stop either event.

When I closed my eyes and slipped towards sleep, I had a nightmare that equaled the evil of Baldur's bad dream. Once or twice I thought I heard rustling outside the window, but I couldn't pull myself out of the dream world. When I finally fell into a deep sleep, my head was full of constantly changing images, skull guests, and floating specters that terrorized me. Snow swirled around, fire burst from the ground. Viking armies battled each other, falling down dead, only to rise up again and continue the fight.

Then the wolf from my other dream returned, loping across the battlefield. But this time, instead of eating me bite by bite, he leapt through the sky and seized the sun, spattering blood across the world. A second smaller wolf swallowed the moon.

Through it all was the sound of scratching, like someone was scraping at a piece of glass with a knife. Or pulling their nails across a chalkboard. And somewhere in the background was my brother's voice, sounding out like a distant bell.

I woke up halfway through the night, sweating like I had run a marathon. I didn't want to fall asleep again because I knew the shapes were still there, somewhere beyond the shadows in my brain, waiting for me. I lay awake, staring at the ceiling, pulling the comforter tight. My arms soon grew tired, my body ached, and, despite my fears, my weary eyelids slid closed. I slept.

"Breakfast!" A loud knock on the door jarred me awake. The lights in the room were on, burning into my eyes. "Breakfast!" Uncle Thordy repeated. "Get up and grab it while it's hot!"

I blinked and sat up. "I thought the plan was to sleep in today."

Sarah was already dressed in jeans and a red lumberjack-type shirt: heavy, warm, but not exactly the height of fashion. She was sitting on the bed pulling her hair into a ponytail.

"Guess the plan changed."

"Well, I need about ten more hours of being zonked out. It's always weird sleeping in a new bed."

"You certainly rolled around a lot last night. I heard you kick the wall a few times." I tried to remember the nightmare again, but couldn't put together enough of the dream to explain anything to Sarah. It was like a big puzzle missing half its pieces. "It's not surprising," Sarah continued. "I don't think our bodies were meant to travel across the Atlantic in less than a day."

I pulled myself out of bed and started digging through my backpack. All my neat packing had been jumbled together during the trip. I tugged out a pair of black jeans that were loose fitting, but didn't make my hips look too big. I slipped them on and wriggled into a dark blue sweater. For some reason my red hair always looked better when I was wearing that color. There was a small mirror on the dresser, so I grabbed my make-up bag and examined myself.

Bags under my eyes. Hair pointing every which way but straight. I looked like I'd spent most of the trip with my head out the airplane window. I did the best I could with my brush.

Sarah's face appeared in the top corner of the mirror, a wicked smile on her lips. "Mordur won't be at the breakfast table," she whispered.

"Oh, please." I stopped teasing my hair long enough to make a face at her.

"I saw the way he looked at you. He kept staring at your hair. Maybe he has a thing for redheads."

"Yeah, right, and maybe I'll get struck by lightning in the next five seconds."

"Hope you brought a lightning rod." She went back to her bed, pulling on some socks.

"What do you suppose is for breakfast?" I asked, changing the topic.

"I don't know for sure, but I can smell it. Eggs and maybe bacon. Hurry up before Michael wolfs it all down."

I gave up on my hair. It would pass for being combed. I

took a moment to pull the curtain aside and glance out the window. Even though my watch read *10:15am*, it was still dark out. What kind of holiday was this going to be if we couldn't see anything?

The window was double paned and I noticed the outside one was etched with three scratch marks. A tuft of gray hair fluttered in the wind, caught in a crack in the wooden sill.

"Sarah, take a look at this."

She came to my side, put her hand on my shoulder. "What's that?"

"It looks like dog hair. How did it get there?"

"I don't know. It's kind of high up for a dog." She stared at it for a moment, pressing her nose up to the glass. "Maybe it was one of those Santa Claus imps — *Gluggagægir*, the window peeper — who came last night."

"And left some hair?"

"I'm kidding," she said, laughing. "I don't know what it's from."

My rumbling stomach stopped me from brooding about it much longer. We went down the hall to the kitchen.

Michael was too busy chewing to say hello, so he just gave us a little wave. Uncle Thordy stood by the oven, a greasy spatula in his hand. Eggs and bacon were frying in a big iron pan, spitting grease across the stovetop.

"Sit. Eat." Uncle Thordy pointed at two empty chairs at one side of a heavy wooden table. The moment we sat down he plunked two plates in front of us and gestured towards a bowl of white stuff. "That's *skyr*," he explained, "made from cow's milk." I'd seen it before. It was like butter but white. Mom and Dad would slather it all over their toast or crackers whenever they could get their hands on some. It tasted much better than it looked. "Dish up!"

Toast was piled on a plate beside a hill of fried eggs and bacon. There were sliced bananas, a box of Kellogg's Corn Flakes, and a selection of cheeses. The cheese was a little old and musty. Maybe that's the way they liked it in Iceland. I dished up and started eating. The eggs had been fried so long that the yolks were solid and the whites partly burnt. The bacon was crisp. Michael was eating a bowl of some steaming porridge-like substance.

"Where's Grandpa?" I asked between mouthfuls.

"He's a little under the weather," Uncle Thordy said, bringing over a pitcher of water. "In fact I'm concerned about him. He's coughing and sweating a lot and has a bit of a fever, but won't let me take him to the doctor. He said he's been tired for the last few weeks, but something really hit him hard last night. He's going to stay in bed today and try to recuperate."

Sarah, Michael, and I exchanged worried glances. "We'll have to check on him after breakfast," Michael said. "Cheer him up with our youthful exuberance."

"I'm sure he'd like that," Uncle Thordy said, "but don't turn on the light. He says his eyes are sore."

We ate quietly for a minute or so. I grabbed a piece of toast and spread some *skyr* across it. "This is a great breakfast."

"I'm glad you like it. It's just so … so nice … to have company out here. Makes me feel safer. I mean, makes the house seem not so empty."

I glanced over at Sarah. She raised one eyebrow.

"I've heard so much about you kids, too," Uncle Thordy continued. "Thursten's very proud of you three. Doesn't stop talking about you. And I know there's something special about you twins."

"Special?" Sarah asked.

Yeah, I wondered. Why were they special?

Uncle Thordy stared straight at Sarah. "You twins have a certain skill for solving problems."

"I don't know what you mean," Sarah said.

"I just … I guess, I'm just trying to say that I know you're good kids, that's all. That we're leaving the family name in good hands."

"Uh, thanks," Michael said.

I wasn't sure if I should be offended. My last name was Laxness, not Asmundson — so I wasn't carrying on their family name. I decided Uncle Thordy wasn't intentionally trying to leave me out. Maybe he'd forgotten my last name.

We ate silently. Uncle Thordy offered us more coffee, but we politely said no. "Aren't you going to eat?" Sarah asked him.

"I had some toast before you got up. I never did much like breakfast. Why don't we say good morning to your grandpa now?"

Grandpa Thursten's room was down a low-ceilinged hallway. The door was made of wooden planks and had a rounded top. It looked ancient.

"It's all that remains of the original house," Uncle Thordy explained. "I had the rest added on about fifteen years ago."

I knocked gently. We waited, but there was no answer. I knocked again, slightly harder, and listened. "Come in," a faint whisper drifted through the wood.

I pushed on the door and it creaked open on a cramped, musty smelling room. The light in the hall lit enough of the room for us to see a chair and a desk, but Grandpa's bed was still hidden by shadows. It took a moment for my eyes to adjust. "Don't just stand around, get in here," a hoarse voice commanded.

I took a few steps with Sarah and Michael right behind me. Grandpa was lying on his side, his head sunk into a pillow, his face pale and pasty-looking, and his eyes dull. The rest of him was hidden under the blankets. He coughed. "I seem to have caught a little bug. I'll be up and at 'em by tomorrow morning. Guaranteed."

I doubted it. I guessed he had a couple days in bed by the way he was looking. Maybe even a week.

"Don't worry," Uncle Thordy said from the doorway. "Mordur promised to show them the croft house and the rest of the farm this morning."

"Good, I wanted them to see the old croft. I spent countless hours out there with my dad. It's where I learned most of the stories I know. It's an important part of our family history."

"I'd take them," Uncle Thordy said, "but unfortunately I have some business to attend to in town. I'll pick up something for supper at the supermarket. A few of the relatives want to drop by tonight. Will you be up for visiting?"

Grandpa answered in Icelandic. Uncle Thordy nodded solemnly, then he forced a smile.

"I'll be ready to give the whole world a good kick in the dustbins," Grandpa whispered and began coughing. I didn't know what to do. We just stood there listening to his painful gasping. Finally I found a glass of water by his bed and handed it to him. "Thanks," he whispered.

"We should let him rest," Uncle Thordy suggested.

I patted Grandpa's open hand. It was clammy. "Angie, stick around for a moment," he rasped. "I want to talk to you about what I got Michael and Sarah for Christmas."

"Sure," I said.

Uncle Thordy put his hands on Sarah and Michael's

shoulders and guided them out of the room, saying, "Guess we better go. It's bad luck to hear what your Christmas present is going to be." He closed the door softly.

"Actually, Angie, I have to ask you something," Grandpa whispered. "It's about the nightmares you had before we left."

» 11 «

"What do you want to know?" My throat felt suddenly dry.

"I'll explain. Just help your ol' grandpa sit up, okay?"

I bent over him, pulling awkwardly on his upper arm until he was in a sitting position. He coughed once more. "Shouldn't you be going to a doctor?"

"This is a minor ailment."

His pillow was out of place, so I tugged on one edge, revealing a small stain of blood. "You're bleeding again."

"It's that pinprick in my back. It itches like crazy. I don't know how I got it." He rubbed the top of his left shoulder and shook his head. "My father would be laughing now. He lost his leg to that bear and not once did he utter a word of complaint. And here I am whining over a mosquito bite." He leaned back. "Could you pass me the water, please?"

I handed him the glass and he slowly sipped a mouthful. "That's better." He gave the glass back and I set it on the bedside table.

I pulled the chair away from the desk and sat next to him. He stared, measuring me with his eyes. "Last night I had the same nightmare as you had when you were back home. A wolf chased me across an open stretch of land. And he devoured me piece by piece."

The wolf wasn't just in *my* head anymore. "How could you have the same dream?" I asked.

"If I follow what I know of psychology, it's just my subconscious acting out the same story you told me. I somehow dreamed a similar dream because you had described yours to me."

"And do you believe that? That you're just … just mimicking me."

He smiled and his face wrinkled up so it looked like old paper. "I've been around a lot longer than most psychologists. I've seen more strange things than the average person. And I've learned to trust my instincts."

"What are they saying?" Each word he spoke was adding to my fear. I didn't want to know any more about that dream, I didn't want to think about it at all.

"The dream is more than just my brain exorcising its demons. It's a sign. A signal. I think it means we should be careful."

"Careful of what? We're safe here, aren't we?" I asked. I couldn't help but think of the fear I had sensed in Uncle Thordy.

"As far as I know, but I … well, years ago, if I was worried, I'd never say anything to you kids. I'd just try and handle it all myself. But now you're older. I have to trust you and let you know what's going on in my brain, even if it sounds crazy. So tell me, do you remember anything else about your nightmare?"

I shook my head, then paused and raised one finger. "Wait, yes, when we were in Hvammstangi I felt like I had been there before. The town was in my dream. I ran through it. And so were the Northern Lights."

"It's almost like you saw the future."

"I don't like to think that. Isn't *deja vu* just a trick your brain plays on you? It could be my imagination. It *has* to be."

"Maybe," he said, sounding doubtful, "but you wouldn't be the first of our clan who's seen something before it happened. Or the last."

I didn't want to know things before they happened. I didn't want *those* kinds of dreams. They always seemed to be about bad things.

"You probably think it's strange to dream of this place," he continued. "I know you were born in North Dakota and raised there, Angie, but this is where you come from. Where all of us Icelanders come from. This is your family's farm."

"I had another dream last night," I admitted, and then explained it to him as best I could.

"Armies that battle each other. A wolf who bites the sun." He counted on his fingers as he spoke. "Another wolf who swallows the moon. That's Skoll and Hati, they've chased the sun and moon for all of time and finally caught them during the final battle between the gods and the giants."

"I dreamed of Ragnarok, Grandpa. Why would I dream of the end of the world?"

He gave a half-hearted shrug. "Don't worry, the world's not coming to an end. It's just about a personal battle, I think. Inside your head. The worst thing about dreams is they aren't meant to be understood by the logical part of our minds. So I don't know if I can make sense of this latest dream. And one thing we should remember is to never completely trust dreams."

I crossed my arms and leaned back in my chair. "What's that mean?"

"Well, for example, I once had a terrible nightmare where I went to a restaurant with your grandma. I ordered a chicken dish, you know that one with Swiss cheese and ham inside. And I choked to death on it. Well, I woke up before I actually died in the dream."

"And have you ever choked on chicken?"

"Not yet. But I refused to eat it. The dream felt so real it had spooked me away from chicken. Your grandma just laughed and after a few months she made me eat a whole plate of fried drumsticks." He chuckled. "It sure was good. But I shouldn't joke. I do think there is something important about your dreams. I just wish I could think straight; my sinuses are aching too much. There is something else bothering me in the real world."

"What?"

Grandpa leaned ahead slightly, speaking more quietly. "Your uncle. He's — I don't know if you can sense it — but he's not right in the head yet. He's still so full of grief over his wife. He forgot to pick us up because he's depressed. Many Icelanders get depressed in the winter, it's so dark for so long. It's only natural. But his sadness is deeper somehow. And he's frightened, too."

"I know. I could tell."

"It's probably just his imagination, that's all. He has a right to feel scared, I guess. His wife died a strange, unexplainable death. Who knows what really happened in that cave." He paused. "You know, I'm starting to sound a little too paranoid. Your grandma always used to say I had more superstition than brains." Grandpa closed his eyes. He had the longest white eyelashes I'd ever seen. "God, I miss her," he said quietly, "I really, really miss her. Sometimes it's so hard to go on without her."

I'd never seen him look so weak, so sad. He'd always been a tower of strength to me. I put my hand on his shoulder and he opened his eyes and smiled. "You've got some of her traits," he whispered. "It's funny, really, we're all like beads on a string following one after another, going on forever. Asmundson after Asmundson."

"And Laxness after Laxness," I added.

"Yes, you're lucky enough to have two strong bloodlines running through your veins." He shook his head. "I do wish I'd paid more attention to your nightmare back home. Maybe I would have called the trip off. I just want you to tell your cousins to be careful. I didn't feel comfortable talking in front of Thordy about this stuff. That's all."

"I'll tell them," I promised. I leaned down and kissed him lightly on the cheek.

"Now I can sleep a little better," he said, closing his eyes.

» 12 «

I found Sarah, Michael, and Uncle Thordy in the living room. Uncle Thordy was standing next to the fire. "I hope you don't mind spending the morning with Mordur," he said. I couldn't think of anything better. "He'll show you around the place. I have a meeting with the banker, otherwise I'd be your guide. I do apologize. I thought you were arriving later today, so I set up appointments in town. That way I'd murder two birds with one rock. I'm so stupid sometimes."

"Uncle Thordy," I said, "you're not stupid. Not at all. You just made a mistake. Back home we call that *pulling a Michael.*"

"Don't even start with me, Angie," Michael warned.

"Pulling a Michael," Uncle Thordy repeated. He furrowed his brow, showing confusion. "I'm not sure what you mean."

"It's a joke," I explained, "like Michael makes mistakes and so we … uh … name mistakes after him."

"Oh, I think I see." Uncle Thordy stroked his beard, pretending to be thinking heavily. "I kind of like that."

"I don't." Michael crossed his arms and feigned anger. "It's deflammatory."

"I think you mean defamatory," Sarah corrected.

"Sorry about that, cuz," I said to Michael, only half meaning it. "I was just trying to … uh …"

"You were just trying to cheer me up," Uncle Thordy finished. "I catch on now." He put his hand on my shoulder, gave it a squeeze. "You're good kids. I wish I could spend the day with you instead of in some stuffy office asking for better interest rates. But that's what being a modern man is all about. Is there anything you need to know before I go? Like where I keep the coffee? Or the cookies?"

"Actually," Sarah said, "I do have a question. What did Grandpa say to you?"

Uncle Thordy frowned, which made the bags under his eyes darken. "When?"

"A few minutes ago," Michael said, "when he spoke to you in Icelandic while we were visiting him. What didn't he want us to know?"

"It wasn't a secret. He was just thanking me for … for taking care of you. And saying it was good to be home. And he reminded me that he was born in that room."

"Born in that room?" I said. "Couldn't they get to the hospital in time?"

"They probably didn't even try. People were pretty independent in those days. Home births were common."

It sounded kind of scary to me. No doctors. No nurses. Just hot water and towels. Grandpa definitely did come from a different time than me. A whole different world. I couldn't imagine sleeping in the same room I was born in.

"I have to get ready to go to town." Uncle Thordy went down the hallway and a moment later we could hear him opening drawers. "Mordur should be here soon," he yelled from his room. "I packed some lunch for your trip. It's in the fridge. Just throw it in the backpack hanging in the closet. It'll be easier to carry."

Someone knocked on the front door.

"Will you get that?" Uncle Thordy shouted.

I suddenly thought of the state of my hair. I wasn't going to answer the door. Not with Mordur on the other side. "Uh, excuse me," I said, making a beeline for the bathroom.

Sarah's voice followed me. "Don't forget to wet down the rooster tail on the back of your head!"

I closed the door to the bathroom, shutting out her and Michael's laughter. I took a good look at myself in the mirror. It wasn't as frightening as I thought it would be. I used a damp facecloth to rub water on my hair, an old trick my mom had taught me. It wets all parts of your hair evenly without soaking it. I found a brush in the cabinet and a few seconds later my red mop looked passable. Even a few curls had shown up. I washed my face and cursed the fact that I'd left my make-up bag in my room.

Michael and Sarah let out a huge guffaw. I hoped they weren't laughing about me. I wiped the facecloth across my face once more. I decided not to worry about my make-up, it was still pretty dark out. I checked my hair for about the fifth time, breathed in, and opened the door.

In the hallway a framed picture caught my eye. It was a large photograph of Uncle Thordy and his wife Kristjanna with mountains in the background. It was hung so that the light in the ceiling lit the image perfectly. Kristjanna was beautiful, a sturdy woman with strong cheekbones and long blonde hair, like she'd walked out of the pages of a saga. And Uncle Thordy, with his arm around her and a smile on his face, looked like a different man. About twenty pounds thinner. No bags below his eyes. His beard trimmed. And no scars above his eyebrow. It nearly brought tears to my eyes, just to see them together. The picture couldn't have been much more than three years old. Uncle Thordy probably stopped and stared at it every day.

Michael, Sarah, and Mordur were standing in the front doorway. I joined them. Mordur was dressed in a thin, gray winter coat. He was an inch or two taller than Michael, with slightly wider shoulders. He smiled at me, showing white, straight teeth. "Ah, Angie, right? Welcome to my group tour. You had good sleep?"

"I did. I had a perfect sleep. One of the best I've had in ages. It sure was a good one."

Sarah gave me a discreet kick, her way of telling me not to babble.

"So no thirteen Santa Clauses visited last night?" Mordur asked. "I am disappointed. I guess you were all good. Any gifts in your shoes?"

"I did find some lint in mine," Michael said. "What does that mean?"

Mordur feigned sadness, wiping away an imaginary tear. "It is going to be a skinny Christmas."

"Lean Christmas," I corrected, softly. "I think that's what you mean."

"Yes." He patted my shoulder. "Thanks. A lean, skinny Christmas for you, Michael. Sorry."

Uncle Thordy came out in fresh clothes, his hair combed back. He smelled like he'd dived into a tub of Brut. Maybe depressed people didn't bathe much.

He winked at us and did up the buttons on his collar. "I've got to make the banker think I'm a dependable businessman."

Mordur spoke to him in Icelandic. It sounded like a question. Uncle Thordy narrowed his eyes slightly, looking a little angry. He snapped three words, glanced at us, regained his composure, and said, "*Bless.*" Which meant good-bye, in Icelandic. And with that he grabbed his coat from the closet, gave us one more wave, and was gone out the door. A moment later his truck started up and roared away.

"What was —" Sarah began to ask.

"No time for talk! Not now!" Mordur said quickly. He seemed to be forcing his lips into a smile, pretending nothing was wrong. "Let's get going. Not much light." He clapped his hands together. "Chop! Chop! Chop it! Dress hot, with big layers. You can peel them off if you get toasted."

Sarah narrowed her eyes, then went to the closet, came out with her thick coat. I grabbed my own and slipped it on, along with my black mittens.

"You'll need something for your head," Sarah reminded Michael.

"Yes, Mom," he said, stuffing his headband into a pocket. A few moments later we were all dressed in our warmest winter clothes, standing at the door.

» 13 «

Mordur escorted us into the yard. It wasn't dark out any more, but it wasn't day either, just some kind of state between the two. There was enough light to turn the snow yellowish. One edge of the sky was brighter than the other, so I assumed that was east. I now saw that Uncle Thordy's farm was in a valley, surrounded by big hills and two rows of cliffs.

"Our lunch!" Michael suddenly exclaimed and rushed back into the house.

"That's Michael, always thinking with his stomach," Sarah said. We laughed.

Remembering the tuft of hair I'd seen earlier in the morning, I walked around the side of the house to our bedroom window. There were tracks in the snow below the sill, but it was hard to tell what had made them. The gray hair I'd seen stuck to the window was more like wool. I picked it up, let it float from my fingers.

It landed beside a small cloth sack that had been bound at the top with a string. The side was ripped open and the contents were gone. There had been something red inside.

"Ready for big tour, Angie?" Mordur shouted. They were already walking across the front yard, away from me.

"Uh … Yes!" I looked down at the bag again, then rushed to join them.

Uncle Thordy's house was the newest part of the farm. The whole yard was an odd mixture of new and old, like there were three different time zones here: kind of old, really old, and ancient. We passed a small, crumbling home, which was about fifty yards from Uncle Thordy's and built into a hill. It was made of wood and sod.

"Do you like my house?" Mordur asked.

"You live in there?" Sarah asked. "Do you have hairy feet?"

"Hairy feet? No." He looked confused. "Why?"

"It's just like a hobbit hole," she explained. "You know, from *The Lord of the Rings*. They were these — uh — little people who had hairy feet. Imps, sort of."

This information didn't end his confusion. "I have simple needs," he said, finally. "I do not own phone. No television, only radio. I like my home. It has history. And my feet are not hairy, I swear."

He flashed a smile and led us through the yard. We stopped in front of a rectangular building with a pitched roof that sagged towards the ground. It had seen more than its share of winters.

"Is this the barn?" I asked. "It's kind of old, isn't it?"

"Why build a new barn?" Mordur said quickly, sounding almost insulted. "This one still stands." It was like I had just asked the stupidest question in all of history. Or perhaps whatever he and Uncle Thordy had quarreled over was still bothering him. "This is more than a barn," he explained, his voice softer, "it is the old home, too. No one is sure when it was built. Uncle Thordy said his grandfather arrived in 1912 and this was here, made by first crofters. It may be two hundred years old and is still strong as the first day it stood." He opened a wide door at one end. "It is our sheep shed now."

He flicked on a switch and four dim bulbs glowed from the ceiling. Inside, huddled against each other, were about fifty sheep, their coats a dirty gray. An overpowering stink of manure hung in the air, accompanied by a feeling of moistness, like all the sheep's exhalations were filling up the barn.

"I assume that's the sweet smell of sheep dip," Michael said, one eyebrow raised. The expression made him look like a really young version of Grandpa. I couldn't help but remember Grandpa's words: *We're all like beads on a string, going on forever, Asmundson after Asmundson.*

"Yes, stinky sheep dip," Mordur answered. "Watch your feet cause it will stick like glue to your boots. This is where our flock winters. The goats and the sheep. They do not get out until after the lambing season at the start of May."

"Not even for a breath of fresh air?" I asked.

"No. Snow comes down hard here. And no warning either. Letting them out during winter is a good way to kill them. Just ask the crofters who were slow with bringing in their flock this fall. They had big problems."

Sarah leaned over to pet one of the sheep. Its coat was so thick it looked like a frizzy ball with matchsticks for legs. "They seem friendly enough."

"They think you will feed them." Mordur led us further

into the barn. The sheep parted and formed into groups, watching us like curious children. There were a few bearded animals, nowhere near as fluffy — goats. It was warm inside the barn, so I unzipped my jacket.

"Hot, right?" Mordur unbuttoned his coat, revealing a thick, gray sweater. "This was home to people back in the old days. Before we got heat from the geothermal pools at Laugarbakki."

"They'd live with their sheep?" Sarah asked.

"And cows. The bunks were right above the cows' stalls. It made smart sense. You keep a good eye on the animals. And they gave off warmth. And you didn't have to walk far to get milk."

I couldn't imagine having to fight my way through a crowd of livestock every time I needed to go outside to the bathroom. It'd be even worse getting ready for a date with all those sheep staring at you.

Mordur opened a gate into another pen. "Wait until you see the old croft house in the far pasture. Compared to it, this barn is heavenly."

"It sounds really *baaaaaaahhhd,*" Michael said, doing his best impression of a sheep.

Sarah looked supremely annoyed. "Even you shouldn't sink so low, Michael."

"Never underestimate how low I will go, sweet sister." Michael bowed.

Mordur took us into the far corner of the barn where two ponies stood, staring at us. "This will be our transport."

Grandpa often spoke glowingly about the Icelandic pony. He called it the most dependable four-legged vehicle in the world. They looked like normal horses compressed into about only two-thirds of the size. One was brown and the other gray, their manes dark and wild, their long tails flowing down to the straw-covered floor.

We helped Mordur bridle the ponies, then led them out into the fresh, open air. They followed without the slightest bit of fuss. "Don't we need saddles?" I asked.

"Bareback riding is not hard. Right, Sleipnir?" Mordur patted the gray pony's forehead. "We will trade turns. It is a long way and there is just four hours of good light, so we had better be quick. I will give you hand up."

He stood beside the pony and cupped his fingers into a stirrup. I'd ridden horses a couple of times before at Michael and Sarah's place, so I knew what to do. I put my left foot in his hand and grabbed the reins. He lifted me carefully and I was surprised at his strength. Then suddenly he lost his footing and slipped to one knee. I fell against him but he was able to hold me up. I had to put my hand on his shoulder to balance myself. "I have got you," he said, gently raising me up again.

The horse stayed perfectly still. I slid my right leg over it, holding the reins in my left hand.

Mordur backed half a step away, keeping one hand on the horse. "Sorry," he said quietly, grinning, "your hair made me — how you say — blinded?"

Was it a compliment? "It does that sometimes," I said and returned his smile.

"You get better grip if you hold the reins in the other hand," he suggested.

"I'm a southpaw. This *is* my best hand."

Mordur gave me a cute but bewildered look. "Southpaw?"

"It means I'm left-handed," I explained, pretending to write with my left hand. "Southpaw is just an expression from back home."

He stared at me blankly. "Well, use either your north or south paw. Just hold tight."

I grinned. Sarah was already on the second horse. She sat up straight and her legs came down past its belly, about two feet from the ground.

"They have seven speeds," Mordur explained, "none very fast. This way." He motioned and started walking towards the hills, with Michael plodding along beside him.

"Giddyup." I shook the reins and the horse paced behind them. I stroked its neck and it raised its head in a sort of salute.

"What are their names again?" I asked.

"That is Sleipnir and the brown is Nonni." Mordur was powering his way through the snow, which was getting deeper the further we got from the buildings.

"Sleipnir?" I said to Sarah, who was riding right beside me. "Isn't that the name of Odin's horse?"

"Yeah, Sleipnir had eight legs and could travel through all the worlds, even down to the underworld." Her ponytail barely bobbed as she rode. It *was* a smooth ride. "Remember the story of how Baldur died from a poisoned dart? And Baldur's brother, Hermod, borrowed Sleipnir and rode all the way to *Niflheim*, the land of the dead. And he begged Hel, the female keeper of the underworld, to let Baldur live again."

"I remember," I said, "that's when Hel said Baldur will only be brought back to life if all the creatures in the world weep for him. But Loki wouldn't shed a tear, so Baldur had to remain in the underworld." I ran my hand across Sleipnir's mane. "There were a couple of other stories about Sleipnir, too, weren't there?"

"Odin races Sleipnir against a giant with a horse named Gold Mane," Michael added, "and he wins hands down."

Mordur was looking at us with open wonderment. "I'm impressive!"

"You're impressed, you mean," I corrected.

He immediately covered his face with one hand, as if to hide his shame. "Yes, I am impressed. You three know a great much about the old myths. And Uncle Thordy said you all are somehow related to Grettir. He is a big hero around here."

"We're Asmundsons through and through," Michael said.

"Except me. I'm a Laxness," I added. "I get my Asmundson blood through my mom. And with a grandfather like ours you have to be able to quote from the myths or the sagas till the cows come home." I paused. "Or should I say till the sheep come home?"

Mordur chuckled, Sarah and Michael groaned. You can't please everyone, I thought. Mordur gave me another of his perfect smiles. There was something about him being out in the open with the landscape all around that made him appear even better looking. He belonged in a painting. "Lax-ness?" he asked. "That is not a common name."

"It was easier to say than Svéinurdarson, our family's original last name. When my great-grandfather landed in Canada, they asked him what his last name was, and he thought they asked him what farm he was from in Iceland. So he said 'Laxness.' And the name has stuck ever since."

We headed through the valley, most of it desolate and covered with a thick layer of snow. Soon the farm was far behind us. The mountains loomed on the horizon, never quite letting us see the sun. The light was so different here than back in North Dakota. It was like being in another world entirely.

"Hey, isn't that Uncle Thordy's truck?" Michael pointed

to the road, which was far below us now. A white truck was parked in a turnoff.

"It is. But I do not see him. Maybe he had a problem," Mordur said, squinting his eyes. "He is close to home. If it is a deflated tire, he will be able to fix it on his own."

We turned and continued on. Soon the hills blocked out our view of the road. Mordur didn't ask to ride either of the ponies, and when I suggested he should take a turn, he said he was used to long walks.

Michael wiped his forehead. "Well *I'm* ready to take a pony for a spin."

I surrendered Sleipnir to Michael, but not before patting the horse on the neck and thanking him for carrying me. Michael launched himself onto Sleipnir's back. He looked rather comical, his legs hanging so low his boots dragged through the snow. "Does this thing have power steering?"

We ignored him and plodded along. Soon we were at the end of the valley and climbing towards a plateau.

"The summer pasture is high up but not far," Mordur explained. After about forty minutes or so, we passed within a few hundred yards of a tiny church set into the side of a hill. A large stone cross stood near the front door like a guardian.

"Who would build a church out here?" Michael asked.

"The old crofters," Mordur said. "There are many churches in Iceland. It was a sign of your goodness to build a church on your land. And wealth."

"Can we go see it?" I asked.

He shook his head. "Not today. Too far long. It looks near, but there are hard paths. And it is high up. It is built so the back overhangs a cliff."

We slogged through the snow. My legs were aching

slightly and my toes felt a little frosty, but it wasn't anything I hadn't experienced before. A little farther on I saw the glint of glass high on a plateau above us. An old, gray house stood on the edge of a large cliff overlooking the ravine. I stopped and pointed at it. "Who lives up there?"

"Gunnvor and her son. That house is made of huge stones. The only stone home in this area. Gunnvor is the one Thordy spoke of last night — very odd, very mean woman. They have no church on their land."

"What's that mean?" Sarah gently pulled back on the reins to get Nonni to stand still.

"There has not been a church built. Their family did not want one. They rarely come down from their place. Who knows what they eat. And when they do show up in town, it is at odd times. Funerals, weddings, town meetings. Always angry and never invited."

"They? How many are there?" Michael asked.

"Gunnvor and her son. Her husband died a long time ago. Gunnvor believes Thordy and his farm are too close to hers, that he is really a sitter — uh — a squatter on their land."

"But hasn't our family owned this place since before the twenties?" I said. "They must have if Grandpa was born here."

"Yes, but Gunnvor's kin were up there lots of years ago. They were first to arrive. They do not care about government-made maps or land titles." Mordur made an odd motion with his hand, like a sign to ward away evil. "I dislike to talk long about them. I get the feelings Gunnvor is staring at us right now." He stepped up his marching speed and led us higher, onto flat land. I kept glancing over my shoulder until the house had disappeared.

"These are the grazing flats." Mordur motioned like a tour guide. From this height the farmhouses were out of sight. The land here was smooth and rounded like the inside of a shallow bowl, made white with snow. "In the spring it is green with grass and marshes and a bright sun. I spend many hours out here watching our flock, daydreaming, reciting the sagas."

"I bet you'd kill for a TV," Michael said.

"There's no reception. It is too far from transmitters," Mordur replied.

"Actually, I was just kidding," Michael said. "A joke."

"Oh, I see … I see it." Mordur grinned. "A TV would be great fun. But I find books far easier to carry."

A chill wind hit us suddenly, whistling over the rock formations and knocking back my hood, making my hair fly all over the place. I tugged the hood back into position.

"We had better get inside," Mordur said. He led us around a large pile of boulders. About twenty yards away, leaning to one side and looking like it had been through several different wars, was the legendary croft house.

» 14 «

It was a lopsided, two-story dwelling that had been built against a hill. The bottom shell was made of wood, and slices of turf were piled against the walls. It looked barely big enough to fit five sheep comfortably. At the top was a rounded loft with a dormer window and a slanted roof thick with snow. Somehow this glorified bunkhouse had stood against all the snow, sleet, and wind nature could throw its way. Crags rose up behind it, dwarfing the place.

Mordur pointed at it. "Here lived one of the first crofters with his sheep, horse, and dogs. And his wife and four children."

"It must have been a tight fit," I said.

"Everyone stayed warm in winter."

"This is what Grandpa wanted us to see?" Michael asked. "A sheep shack?"

Mordur pulled back his hood. "This *sheep shack* has bigger history than some castles. It is what Iceland is about — people working hard to make a living. Fighting against snow, rain, bad prices. The real Iceland heroes are the old crofters. They deserve respect. Your family is part of this croft house's story. Your grandfather spent his childhood summers up here."

"I bet all he did was talk to himself and make up bad jokes," Sarah said.

The wind had doubled, whipping my hair against the side of my face. I pulled my neck scarf tighter. "Will this place keep us warm?" I asked.

"It will block the breeze." If Mordur thought this was a breeze, I'd hate to see his idea of a storm. He led us closer. "I stayed up here most of last fall watching the flock. It is a good shelter." The front door was big enough for a cow to go through. Mordur yanked the door open and it nearly fell off. It was hanging by one rusted hinge. Michael and Sarah had dismounted and were about to tie the horses to an old post. "No, bring them in," Mordur said, holding the door wide. "This is where they stay."

We led the horses into a cramped space that was half a foot taller than their heads. We had to stoop to enter. The air was stale; cobwebs hung down from the ceiling. Two stalls stood along one wall. Mordur gestured. "There were maybe twenty lambs and two horses here in the old days."

"They must have stacked them," Sarah said, pulling Nonni further into the stable.

"Stack them?" Mordur gave her a quizzical look. "Oh, I see, no — they just squish them together. They were plenty happy when spring came."

"Where's the rest of the place?" Michael asked. "You don't sleep on this straw in the summer do you?"

Mordur motioned above us. "Follow me."

He took the reins of both horses and tied them in separate stalls. The wind whistled between cracks, stirring the dust and the old straw. It was going to be a long, cold walk home. Of course, if it was gusting in the right direction it might push us all the way back to Uncle Thordy's house.

Mordur stopped at a seven-runged ladder that led to the ceiling. He climbed to the top, pushed on a corner, and a trapdoor opened. "Climb up," he said.

Michael went first. Sarah brushed a cobweb off her shoulder. "This is not what I expected from a European vacation."

"I was hoping for a dip in one of those famous Icelandic hot springs, myself," I said.

Sarah laughed, then turned and started up. By the time I got to the top, Mordur had already lit an oil lamp and had set it in the middle of the room on a metal stove. The place stunk of must and dry manure. There was a washbasin imbedded in one wall and three sleeping benches stuck out from another. There wouldn't have been much privacy. An old, lumpy-looking mattress rested on the middle bench. A table, slightly larger than a newspaper, was nailed below a windowsill. The shutters were latched closed, but the "breeze" was still trying to force its way in, rattling them.

Sarah sat on a bench. "A whole family would stay up here?"

"They must have been pretty short," Michael said.

"They were good benders." Mordur was hunched over, dragging a wood chair across the floor. "Icelanders are smarter than most people think. Let's lunch."

I headed towards one of the wood benches, avoiding the grungy mattress. My foot kicked a small object and I looked down. A dead mouse. "Gross," I said, jumping away.

I knocked over something. It was a slim wooden box about ten inches long. It broke open on the floor and three rolled-up pieces of paper fell out.

"What're you doing, Angie?" Michael was sitting on a three-legged stool, one hand under his chin like he was thinking real hard. "Some kind of new dance?"

"I just about stepped on that dead mouse."

"There is a lot here." Mordur didn't sound too worried. "They like this place."

I was going to be extremely careful where I sat. But first, I picked up the paper scrolls and partly unrolled one, revealing lines of writing. The paper was quite thick and felt rough around the edges. "What are these made of?"

"Calfskins," Mordur answered.

"Yuck!" I dropped them right away. This place was a junkyard. I'd probably caught a hundred diseases in the last few seconds. "What on earth are they doing here?"

He grinned. "They belonged to my father. In the old days the Icelanders would not have much paper — not enough trees — so they wrote stories on dried and stretched calfskins. Dad liked to study history of crofters, so he made these on his own. This is how sagas were preserved."

I picked one up gingerly and looked at the words. "They're in French. Are they ... uh ... a diary?"

"I cannot read it. Dad spent some years working on a French fishing troller and lived in Paris. He met my mother there. These letters might be to her, but he and her were — uh — how do you say it? Not good company together."

"We know what you mean," Sarah said softly.

"If they're not for your mom," Michael asked, "then why are they in French?"

Mordur shrugged. "Maybe he wanted to keep them secret. Not many Icelanders know French."

"What are they doing in the croft house?" Sarah asked.

"They were a big hobby of my father while he watched the sheep. I found the skins last fall in the walls when I set mousetraps."

"I don't think they're a diary," I said, scanning them. "They might be a story."

"Why?" Mordur asked.

"I recognize one word: *loup-garou*. It means werewolf. Was your dad a writer?"

"He did tell tales. Maybe he wrote some down." Mordur took the calfskins from me, looked at them for a moment, then rolled them back up. "There is another thing," he said and reached into a corner of the box and pulled out a long slender metal object. It had four sharp edges that tapered down to a point and was about twice the length of my index finger.

Michael brought his chair closer. "Is that a spearhead?"

"Yes. There are tiny figures carving into it. I think Dad made it, too. There is a drawing of the spearhead on one of the calfskins."

"He was a talented guy," I said.

"Yes," Mordur agreed, "he had lots of big projects. He wished to be known as the crofter who made the old days come to life."

"'Cattle die,'" I quoted, "'kinsmen die, I myself shall die, but there is one thing I know never dies: the reputation we leave behind at our death.'"

"Why did you say that?" Mordur asked.

"It's something our grandfather taught us, from a story about our great-grandfather," I explained. "I guess I just wanted to say it looks like your dad succeeded. He's created some real beautiful things. I'm sure people around here remember him as a historian. This stuff should be in a museum."

Mordur nodded. "You are right. One thing we Icelanders worry about always — what people will think about us after we are gone."

"I bet Grandpa can read the calfskins," Michael said. "He's from Canada. I'm sure he knows a few words in French. I remember him translating the French on a cereal box for me once."

"I will show him then." Mordur carefully placed the calfskins and the spearhead inside the wooden box and clasped the lid shut.

The gusting wind picked up outside, rattling the sides of the croft house. Drafts of cold air crept across the floor, rose high enough to make the flame in the oil lamp flicker. The place wasn't exactly windproof.

Michael opened up our lunch and grabbed some *hardfiskur*. He passed the bag to us. I took an apple and a strip of the dried fish. Even in the dim light of the oil lamp, the fish didn't look all that yummy. I handed the remainder to Sarah. "I have a question," Sarah said to Mordur. "It's about Uncle Thordy. And if you don't want to answer it, I'll understand."

Mordur was silent for a few seconds, his face serious.

"I answer what I can. But remember, he is my boss *and* my friend. He has done much for me."

"I understand," Sarah said. She bit her lip, thought for a second. "When we first arrived, he seemed … I don't know … frightened. Like he expected something bad to happen. Do you know why?"

"He has not been good since Kristjanna died. It is over a year and a half. Before that Thordy made the jokes and

would whistle while he worked. He is all nerves now. He …
I don't know how much I should let spill."

"He's family," Sarah said softly. She briefly held Mordur's
hand, which made me raise an eyebrow. "We want to help
him if we can."

"Well, he sometimes goes into deep sadnesses. He stays
in the house for lots of days, leaves the lights off. He told
me I was never to go in, unless he lets me in. Other times he
leaves for a week without telling me. It is like he is trying to
go away from everything. And I do not complain, but I do
most of the work now. I rounded up all the sheep on my
own last year. And there are troubles with money."

"Is that why he's going to town today?" Michael asked.

"Yes. Thordy wants another loan to keep the farm going on. He is not good with the books. He used to be most
good. But what is going on in his head is what really bothers me. Sometimes I see his shadow in the window, staring
out at the yard for hours, waiting for something to appear."

"But maybe there's some other reason for it. Did someone rob the place?" I asked.

"No, nothing like that. Part of it is a little — uh — bad
thing we have been having on the croft. It started after
Kristjanna's death. We lost two kids."

"You mean kids have died?" I asked.

"He means baby *goats*, Einstein," Michael explained,
rolling his eyes.

"Uh … I'll shut up now." I took a nervous bite of the
hardfiskur. It was as hard as it sounded, but not bad once you
chewed it for awhile. I swallowed, and the lump scraped its
way down my throat.

"These goats disappeared without trace. We knew they
were gone, because their mothers made such a noise. It is a

terrible sound when a mother goat loses her kid. It upsets the whole flock.

"Thordy and I split up and looked low and high for them. My dog Tyr and I stumbled across their remains. They had been dragged onto a rock shelter high above the plain, their bones spread across the ground and broken in half. All the marrow was sucked out. The flesh was eaten."

I felt cold. I slipped my hands inside my jacket pockets. Mordur was staring into the flame of the lamp, looking hypnotized. "Thordy was not happy. We called the local constable and tried to figure what did this. Not a fox. And men are the only other meat eaters on Iceland. There were rumors about a mountain man — a criminal who lives in hiding — but the tooth marks were too sharp."

"Nothing more happened for months, and we got the sheep safely home, but that winter was *fellivetur*, a slaughter winter. Deep snow. Very cold. In the old days they had to kill all livestock because they would have nothing to feed them.

"On one evening when the moon was high and bright, I was out shoveling off my roof. It had just snowed. I stopped to rest and heard Tyr bark a warning. I climbed down and real fast made my way out into the deep snow. But his barking got far and farther away. Then it became growling and yelping and finally he was silent. I ran quick through hip-deep snow, the moon showing me my way. I rounded a corner and saw a big, gray thing feeding on the body of Tyr. It looked up at me. Its eyes glowed with orange light. They held me and I could not move, a cold chill going through my bones. The creature backed away, seemed to almost smile. Then it ran off into the night."

He stopped. The wind continued to buffet the croft

house, shaking the shutters. It wasn't getting any warmer inside.

"Has anything else happened since?" Michael asked.

"Two more lambs died. We did not find their bones. But they were safe in the barn before they disappeared."

"What do you think it was?" I asked.

"Maybe just a wolf that rode an ice floe here. About every twenty years one shows up. I do not know how it got in our barn, though. There are no holes wide enough. Thordy and I spent the summer patching. And it could not open the latch; you would need hands for that."

"You didn't want to bring us out here, did you?" Sarah was using *the stare*, the one where she knows there's an answer, and if she stares long and hard enough you'll spit it out.

"What?" Mordur looked stunned by the question.

"That's what you and Uncle Thordy argued about before we left." She kept staring at him.

He pursed his lips. "Yes, we had a disagree. I … I wasn't sure if it was safe. He said it was daylight, there was no thing to fear …"

The window shutter banged open as if a fist had struck it. A blast of snow and biting wind swept over us. Mordur struggled towards the window. He grabbed the shutters and was able to close one, but not the other. Michael jumped up beside him, pushing on the second shutter until Mordur could latch them both shut. With Michael's help he jammed a post against them. "It is really storming big. I could not see much past the window. This was not in any of the radio forecasts."

The sudden chill had knocked the last bit of warmth from my body. "Let's go home. I don't want to be stuck out here for Christmas."

Mordur peered through the cracks. "We had better wait. It is a whiteout. The paths would be very not good. It will blow by soon. Of course, if you do not like the weather now, just wait five minutes, it will get worse."

"What?" Michael said.

"It is a saying. A joke. We will be okay. And Thordy knows where we are. The world would not end if we stayed the night."

"It'd be pretty close," Sarah whispered. I wrapped my arms around myself.

"Why not start a fire?" Mordur opened the grate on the stove. He carried an armful of what looked like brown squares from a pile by the wall and threw them in the pot belly. Then he took a hand shovel full of gray-black chunks from another pile and tossed them inside.

"What's that?" Michael asked.

Mordur lit a match. "Peat. I dug it up from the marshes east of the house. And dried sheep's dung. It burns good." He tossed the match in and seconds later a fire appeared. "Logs are hard to find up here."

"Is it gonna stink?" I asked.

"You will get used to it."

Yeah right, I thought. At first I stayed as far away as I could, but soon the stove began to cast off heat, so Sarah and I edged closer, holding our hands near the stove, letting our palms grow warm.

There was a grating sound from downstairs. Then a slam. The horses whinnied loudly and banged around inside their stalls.

Michael looked up from the fire, eyes wide. "What the heck was that?"

» 15 «

We listened for what seemed an eternity. The wind continued to hiss through the cracks, but I couldn't hear anything else. Michael took a step towards the trapdoor and the floorboards creaked below his feet. Mordur motioned him to be still.

The beams that held up the croft house began groaning. The sound became louder and harsher and I realized it wasn't the beams making the noise. It was something else. A growl reverberated somewhere below us.

"There's something down there," Sarah whispered.

The growl grew deeper. It was unlike anything I'd ever heard. It worked its way into my nerves, my bones, my spine so that I couldn't move.

The others were frozen in place too, all straining to hear the next noise. The flames in the stove died down and a coldness crept into the room. Even the oil lamp grew dimmer.

The horses had remained silent and I imagined them pressed up against the sides of their stalls, tied tightly, eyes wide with fear, not wanting to attract the attention of the intruder.

Mordur reached for the fire poker and gripped it tightly. "We should not have come here." He took a step towards the trapdoor, then stopped as if he wasn't sure what to do next.

The growling grew louder. The support beam in the center of the croft house creaked like a weight had leaned up against it. A heavy hissing noise drifted through the floor-boards.

I came slowly out of my shock. There were cracks in the floor, so I knelt and looked through one. It was dark down there, except for a frail band of light.

I could make out a thin shape next to the support beam. It wasn't that large, maybe four or five feet tall. It was stand-ing on its hind feet and appeared to be covered with fur. Its head was hidden in shadows. It was definitely some kind of animal, but not one I recognized.

"I ... I think I see it," I whispered.

It turned towards me, as if it had heard my voice, and revealed a long snout.

"What ..." Michael began. I looked up, motioned him to be silent.

I peeked back down and the thing had moved out of the pale light.

One of the horses neighed sharply, then the other. A board snapped. A roar, this time so loud it drowned out the horses' cries, echoed through the floor. A second timber broke, then came the clomping of hooves, a crash.

A large dark blur shot through the band of light — one of the horses. He smacked into the side of the croft house.

The neighing of both horses became louder, higher-pitched, so that they weren't even the noises of horses anymore. They sounded almost human, like they were being tortured.

Then there was a thud. Now there was only one horse neighing, its voice ragged. It wheezed out its fright, stomping and struggling against an unseen attacker. Roars and growls echoed through the trapdoor.

For a moment the horse stood in the light and I could see its gray hide. It was Sleipnir. Four gashes stretched along his side; one leg looked broken. He tried to neigh, but only blood bubbled out of his mouth.

A gray shape jumped onto his back and clung to him. Sleipnir let out a frightened, gurgling whinny, kicked up his front legs, and jumped out of the light. The whole croft house shook.

We looked at each other. Mordur was still holding tightly to the fire poker. Michael, who had been frozen in place, shifted his weight and the floor creaked, loudly. There was an answering rustle from below us. Then came an odd, child-like cry of discovery from a few feet below the trapdoor. Like a prize had been found.

Us.

» 16 «

The ladder creaked as rung by rung the intruder climbed up. Next came a sniffing, a great inhalation of air. This was a hunter who had tasted blood and now wanted more. There wasn't a nerve in my body that would function. Ice ran through every vein, weighing me down.

We stared at the trapdoor. It lifted slowly, hinges squeaking with rust. A snout tested the air for several seconds, then the thing pushed its head up into the chamber and turned towards us, its eyes glowing orange. The creature looked human, except for the protruding canine snout and a covering of dark gray fur. It opened a wolf-like mouth and let out a low growl. Dangling from its teeth was a strip of hide, flesh still attached.

It brought up a hand, not a paw, but a hand — with four clawed fingers and a thumb.

Before it could climb another step, Mordur yelled,

launched himself through the air, and landed on the trapdoor, knocking the beast to the ground with a great thump. It roared and a second later the trapdoor, which Mordur was still lying across, was struck from below, lifting it up a few inches and nearly throwing Mordur right off.

"Help me hold it down!" he cried.

Michael got there first, kneeled next to Mordur, adding his weight to the door. I forced each muscle into motion, stood up. The trapdoor was hit a second time and one of the hinges flew into the air, deflecting off the roof.

I found a long post and slid it across the door, between Michael and Mordur. There were two rings on either side that had been nailed into the floor. Sarah grabbed the other end of the post and helped me guide it towards the opposite ring, but it was too big to fit cleanly.

A third blow hammered into the wood. Michael was knocked off and Mordur fell away, clutching his ribs.

"Quick!" Sarah hissed. "Push it through."

I shoved the post. It caught the other ring and I forced it into the hole, blocking the door. Michael and Mordur had jumped back on the door, braced themselves for an impact.

None came.

There was a knothole in the center of the trapdoor, large enough to see through. I leaned over to peer through it and was hit by a scent of rotting flesh. Then a large, hypnotizing eye filled the hole, swirling with orange and gray colors. It mesmerized me. A voice began to speak in my head in a language I'd never heard before. But the message was clear: *Surrender. Don't struggle. Don't resist. There is no escape.* The eye stared right into me, seemed to know who I was. My body became weak.

"Annnngggie." Michael's voice sounded slow and thick. "Annngie whatttsss wwrrronngg?"

Someone leaned in beside me. Sarah. Close enough that she could see through the hole. She gasped, then backed away. "Geh-eh-ttt gonnnne!" she yelled. Her voice freed me slightly and I was able to inch away. She had stoked the fire, lighting the room, and was now holding a heated metal poker. "Get gone!" she commanded. *"Fardu burt! Draugr! Flydu!"*

She ran forward and shoved the poker down into the knothole. The thing below us screamed and pounded so hard against the trapdoor that the wood cracked. Another wail followed, like a child that had been denied a toy.

We could hear the creature running and the noise of the door to the outside crashing open.

Sarah lowered the poker.

"Is it gone?" Michael asked. "Is it gone?"

I slowly released my grip on the post. My body ached. I bent and peeked through the crack in the trapdoor, afraid I would see that eye again, hear that voice. But there was nothing. Snow was blowing in through the door; already a small bank had formed on the ground.

"What the hell was that?" Michael asked.

"It was … it was …" I was shaking, my hands cold. "I thought it only went after sheep, Mordur."

Mordur was still kneeling on the trapdoor, holding his ribs. He pushed himself to his feet. "That was not what attacked my dog. That was too small."

"You mean there's something larger out there?" I asked.

"I do not know. Perhaps," Mordur said.

"Well, that's great news," Michael said. He looked at Sarah. "And what were *you* yelling? Some kind of hocus pocus?"

Sarah shook her head. "It was from the sagas. I read it a long time ago. It just came back to me before I hit that thing in the eye."

"Well, it worked," Mordur said, "but for how long?"

» 17 «

We armed ourselves with whatever we could lay our hands on — Mordur found a large hunting knife, Michael a board, Sarah kept the metal poker. I picked up a walking stick. We waited, listened. When we finally thought it was safe, Michael slid the pole out of the rings and slowly lifted the trapdoor. Mordur leaned into the hole, craned his neck so he could see into all corners of the lower croft room. "It is gone," he said. He climbed down the ladder, holding the knife in one hand. Michael, then Sarah, followed.

I decided the walking stick was too thin for a weapon, so I searched around for something else.

"Angie, what're you doing up there?" Michael yelled through the trapdoor.

"I'll be down in a second." I found another fire poker leaning against a chair, and next to it the backpack that Michael had used to carry our lunch. A few inches away was the box of calfskins. It seemed to be my job to clean up after these guys. I gently put the box inside the backpack and pulled it over one shoulder. I grabbed the poker and went to the stove, twisting a key on the oil lamp. The wick sank out of sight, the light died. I stumbled across the floor to the trapdoor and climbed down the ladder.

The front door had been knocked off its hinges; snow blanketed the ground floor. Mordur was bent over one of the horses. "Poor Sleipnir. Look at his throat …"

Sarah turned away. "It's terrible." I was glad to be standing a few feet away, I couldn't see anything clearly.

Mordur stared at Sleipnir, his face grim. "Thordy and I will come back to bury them. They will be good here for now. With the snow and cold."

Mordur stood up and stared out the entrance, holding his knife out in front of himself. "I do not think that … that thing will be back soon. It will be holed up somewhere with a sore eye. The snow is cleared, maybe enough to make home. Are you ready to go?"

"We don't have much choice," Michael said. Sarah was already tightening a scarf around her face. I pulled my zipper up. I didn't want to spend another moment in this place.

We entered a world of whiteness. There was a splash of red next to the broken door. I stepped closer and found a small cloth sack on the ground, just like the one I'd seen back at Uncle Thordy's house. It had been torn open and a black liver-like thing sat on the snow.

"What's that?" I asked.

"Butcher bag," Mordur said. "Livers and hearts and organs. For fox traps."

"I saw a bag like that near the house," I said. "What's another one doing here?"

He shrugged. "I do not know. But we better go home."

We marched through the snow, which had now gathered into huge drifts. The occasional blast of wind tried to knock us off our feet and coated our eyebrows and scarves with wet snow. We struggled through high banks, frosty air rising from our mouths. I had no idea what time it was anymore. The light behind us was fading.

On the plateau, the snow made everything look even flatter. There was no horizon, just a blank world. Somehow Mordur found the way. We traveled in single file, one step behind him. He would turn to help when there was a long drop or a difficult area to cross.

We hardly spoke. Sarah stumbled and Michael let her lean on his shoulder. They walked this way for quite awhile, helping each other. I thought of Andrew and what it would be like if he were still here. Tears welled up in my eyes.

I was growing colder and rubbed my cheeks to get the blood flowing, then tightened up my scarf.

Mordur halted every once in awhile and searched around as if trying to see some invisible pursuer. I sped up so I was a step behind him. "I got your dad's letters," I yelled above the wind.

"Did you?" He looked surprised and relieved. "I forgot them from my mind."

"I knew you'd want them." I wanted to say something else. Something about his father perhaps. Maybe I'd tell him I knew what it was like to miss someone you cared about.

Mordur cast another glance backwards, but before I could open my mouth to tell him what I was thinking, he shouted, "Hurry! Soon there will not be any light left."

The sky was now gray. How long had we been out here? I picked up my pace, gave up on talking. Every ounce of energy was funneled towards putting one leg in front of the other. I couldn't help but think that there was something in the snow behind us, pursuing us.

The feeling of running away reminded me of my nightmares. Were they warnings about what attacked us in the croft house? Or was there something worse out there?

When I first spotted Uncle Thordy's house, I let out a small cheer. The porch light flickered and Uncle Thordy's truck was parked outside. We broke into a run, kicking snow ahead of us.

We burst into the house without knocking. Uncle Thordy met us in the hall, his fists clenched. "You're back!" he exclaimed, dropping his hands. "Are you all right?"

At first none of us spoke. Whatever he saw in our faces must have answered his question. "What happened?" He looked directly at Mordur. "What happened?"

"The *úlfslikid*, it attacked us."

» 18 «

Uncle Thordy's eyes widened. "During the day! Where?"

"In the croft ..." Mordur began. He sucked in some air, held his side. "I ... I think we must sit down."

"Come in, come in." Uncle Thordy motioned with his hands. "You all look like you've been dragged through *Niflheim* and back."

We kicked our boots off, dropped our weapons, and tumbled into the living room. Uncle Thordy locked the door and followed us. The lights of the Christmas tree reflected in the window and the fireplace was blazing. It looked like heaven. I collapsed on the easy chair and loosened my jacket. I set the backpack at my feet. Michael and Sarah plopped down on the couch, both still dressed for outside. Mordur leaned against the wall beside me, favoring his right side.

"You okay?" I asked.

"Yes," he wheezed, "just a little bump."

"Why don't you sit?" I said, patting the armrest of my chair.

He gave me a mocking salute that only made him wince more, then sat carefully. "Thanks," he whispered.

Uncle Thordy had gone into the kitchen. He returned with a tray full of coffee in huge gray mugs. I grabbed mine eagerly, the comforting smell filling my nostrils. I sipped. It almost burned my tongue.

"Where are the horses?" Uncle Thordy asked.

"Dead." Mordur leaned one arm on his knee, trying to take pressure off his chest. "Both dead."

There was the sound of a door opening and footsteps plodding down the hall. Grandpa stumbled like a sleepwalker into the room, his face as pale as the white bathrobe he was wearing.

"Uncle Thursten, careful." Uncle Thordy got up and tried to guide him to a seat, but Grandpa just waved him away. Step by slow, careful step he closed in on his target, then turned and lowered himself onto the couch beside Sarah. He looked like he'd aged ten years in the last ten hours. His eyes were bloodshot. His lips curled into a painful smile. "Don't stop on my account," he whispered hoarsely, "things were just getting interesting. Please, though, for an old man's sake, start at the beginning."

So we did. First Mordur spoke, then we found our voices. Sarah would explain something and Michael and I would add our bits. It was a jumbled story, like piecing together a nightmare. I drank the rest of my coffee; my body was finally starting to warm up. I took my jacket off.

When we finished, Grandpa cleared his throat. It was a gross, phlegmy sound. He looked at Mordur. "So you think this — we'll call it a wolf — is different than the one you saw before?"

"Yes. But it was dark both times. Maybe it grew large in my memory."

Grandpa thought this over for a second, then turned to Uncle Thordy. "How many attacks have there been?"

"Four," Uncle Thordy said. "Just on animals though. The only evidence we've found are tracks."

"Wolf tracks?"

"No, not exactly. They are larger. But signs of claws in the print. They always disappear after a few hundred yards. And, up until now, it's only happened at night. Dogs won't follow the beast, they just spin in circles and yelp. The constable is baffled by them." Uncle Thordy wiped sweat from his forehead. The thick scars above his eyebrow glistened. "I thought the nephews would be safe. I'd never have allowed a trip to the old croft house if I thought this could happen."

"It wasn't like anything I'd seen before," I said, thinking of its glowing eyes. "It climbed the ladder. It had … hands."

"Hands?" Uncle Thordy repeated.

"Did it bite any of you?" Grandpa asked.

We all shook our heads.

"Any scratches?"

Again, we shook our heads. Grandpa let out his breath, like we'd answered an important question.

My thoughts were getting tangled. I wanted to yell *What's going on?* Grandpa seemed to know more than he was letting on. Maybe Uncle Thordy did, too.

Another part of me just wanted to curl up in some corner and hide. Too much was happening.

"I …" Mordur began. "I have a favor to ask from you, Mr. Asmundson."

"It's Thursten," Grandpa said. "And what's this favor?"

Mordur reached down for the backpack, opened it, and pulled out the box. He lifted the lid and gently took out the calfskins. "These were hidden in the croft house. My father wrote French on them. Michael said you would read it."

"French?" Grandpa echoed. "I can't say I know much of it. My wife dragged me to a French class for a few months before we went on a holiday in Quebec. I watch hockey games on the French channel, but that's about it. At least I know when they say, 'he shoots, he scores.' I'll give it a try."

"There is also this." Mordur held the spearhead in the palm of his hand so everyone could see. It glinted in the light. "I think Dad made it."

"He kept himself busy," Uncle Thordy said. "That's one thing about Einar. If he wasn't reading some old book about Icelandic history, he was trying to recreate it. Some of the professors at the university would even phone him and ask him questions. He showed me a paper that one professor had written that quoted him. He was pretty proud of that."

"May I hold it?" Grandpa said, and Mordur handed the spearhead to him. "That's a fine piece of metalwork. Light, sharp as a razor. And all these symbols carved on the sides. This must have taken a long time." He gave the spearhead back. "I wish I could have met your father. He sounds like quite the man."

"He was," Mordur said.

Just then I saw the slightest movement in the kitchen window.

There was a face staring in at us.

Then it was gone.

"There's someone outside," I said.

"What?" Uncle Thordy turned towards the kitchen, following my gaze. "Where?"

"In the window," I answered, my voice cracking. "Just for a second. Someone looked in."

Uncle Thordy got up, went into the kitchen. Michael and Mordur followed. They stood at the window peering through the glass.

"Th-there," Sarah whispered. She was still seated next to Grandpa, pointing at the window in the living room. "Someone's there."

I turned. Glaring through the pane was an old, female face, eyeballs the size of boiled eggs, glaring from me to Sarah to Grandpa. The reflection of the Christmas tree lights made it seem like the woman was looking in at us from another world.

The old woman's scratchy voice carried through the windowpane. She was shouting in Icelandic.

"It's Gunnvor," Uncle Thordy whispered, amazement in his voice. "I haven't seen her for years."

The name sounded familiar. Then I remembered Grandpa had talked about the old woman who lived on the hill. Only hours ago we'd seen her stone house at a distance. So this was Gunnvor.

"She says she's lost her child," Grandpa said. "She says we stole him."

Uncle Thordy strode further into the living room. "Gunnvor," he said loudly, as if he was speaking to someone who was hard of hearing. He shouted something in Icelandic and pointed to the front door.

Gunnvor seemed to grunt a reply.

Uncle Thordy raised his voice even louder, repeated the words.

She disappeared from the window.

We followed Uncle Thordy to the front door. He opened it and called Gunnvor's name a few times, then muttered under his breath like he was cursing. "Mordur, get the flashlights from the kitchen. I'll need help to find her."

Mordur went towards the kitchen, grimacing like he was trying to hold in the pain. Maybe his ribs were broken.

Sarah was already pulling on her coat and heading for the door. "I'll help."

"I'll hold down the fort," Grandpa said from his seat.

I wasn't sure if I wanted to go outside. The woman didn't look all that friendly. And who knew what else could be out there? Michael went out the door too, so I pulled on my jacket and, as I did, noticed a tear in the shoulder. Perhaps I'd caught it on something in the croft. It felt like a bad omen.

We filed out into the front yard. The snow had stopped

and there wasn't a breath of wind. The Northern Lights were back, dancing like angels through the sky. We circled the house, but the only sign of Gunnvor was a sled she had left next to the fence.

"There," Mordur said, pointing his flashlight towards the barn.

I could just make out Gunnvor past Uncle Thordy's shoulder. She was wrapped in a large fur coat and crouched in the beam of the flashlight. She wore a cloth cap, but her long gray hair was loose and falling past her shoulders. She glared at us, then pushed open a gate and trudged towards the barn, moving pretty fast for someone who looked older than Iceland itself. Had she walked all the way here from her home?

Sarah must have come to the same conclusion. "I think that's one tough ol' woman," she whispered.

"Gunnvor!" Uncle Thordy yelled. "Wait!"

She grunted something over her shoulder.

"She's going into the barn," Uncle Thordy said, anger in his voice. "She's going to frighten all the sheep. The crazy old hag. Why won't she stay where she belongs?"

He stormed off to the barn, flicked on the lights. We followed him through the front door. The sheep were gathered in one corner, huddled against each other, looking at us, their legs shaking.

Michael closed the door and we walked to the far end of the barn, passing through a gate. There was a large pile of straw in the middle of a stall. Gunnvor was on her knees, throwing handfuls of it behind her. A soft whimpering sound came out of the pile.

We stood back as first a leg appeared, then another, then a chest and arms, and finally the face of a boy, maybe ten years old. His features were wild with terror, and both his eyes were bruised and swelling. He was foaming at the mouth and holding up his hands to block the light. Strips of clothing covered him and there were scratches on his chest, arms, and cheeks. Dried blood stained his body.

"He's been mauled," I said. "He looks awful."

"Scratches," Gunnvor barked over her shoulder in a thick accented English. She turned back, whispered softly in an almost singsong voice completely unlike her previous gruntings. *"Onni. Onni. Onni."*

How could such an old woman be his mother?

"What is wrong?" Mordur asked. "What happened?"

Gunnvor turned her head. "He wanders. He is feeble-minded." She stared daggers at Mordur. "I know you. Einar's brat. Snoopy as your father. Look where it got him."

Mordur didn't flinch. "How did your son get those scratches?"

"Not your business, whelp," she hissed. She cast her eyes to Michael, Sarah, and me. "And stop staring at me. You smell of the New World. Thorgeir Tree-Foot's little brood comes back to stink up the farm." She turned to her son.

A light of recognition came into Onni's eyes. He suddenly reached out and with a sharp cry and sigh flung his arms around Gunnvor's neck. She lifted him from the straw. I saw a mean-looking gash below his right eye.

A cloth bag fell from his hands. It was torn open, and something that looked like liver slipped out onto the floor. Just like the bags I'd seen earlier in the day.

Gunnvor kicked at the contents. "Who baited him?" Her eyes were blazing with rage now. I edged back, afraid of what I saw in her. "Which one of you?"

No one spoke. I looked at the ground to avoid her glare.

"One of you did," she said. "I would crush your bones if I knew which one." I didn't doubt her. There was steel in her words. Her skin was wrinkled and her gray hair wild about her shoulders, but her thick body looked strong. "If this is one of your tricks, Thordy, you will pay." She pointed a pudgy finger at him, still clutching Onni in her arms. Uncle Thordy straightened his back and narrowed his eyes like he was getting ready for a fight. "You try to cover up your scent with perfumes, but you cannot hide from me." She spat at him, then strode past us, through the gate and out of the barn.

"We can help you," Uncle Thordy said, running after her. We followed.

"No help, not from you," Gunnvor grunted. "Just home. Away from your kind." She carried Onni to the sleigh and wrapped him in blankets. He had calmed down. His eyes stared listlessly at the sky.

"You can't drag him all the way home," Uncle Thordy said, taking a step toward her, then stopping himself, as if he feared she would lash out at him. "Not through all this snow. Please, come inside, we can look after his wounds."

"This isn't enough snow to bother a *real* valley dweller." She pulled on a rope, tying her son to the sleigh.

"But …" Uncle Thordy began.

"*No,*" Gunnvor said, sharply. She began dragging the sleigh, each stride long and solid. She headed into the east, the Northern Lights swirling above her.

» 20 «

A slight breeze was stirring. Clouds had filled in the edges of the sky. Large flakes of snow started falling, getting thicker by the moment. The worst part of the storm may have passed, but Old Man Winter wasn't done dumping snow on us.

We went back inside the house. Grandpa was still in his seat, coughing so hard his face had turned red. Sarah quickly brought him water and he thanked her before tipping back the glass. I sat in the same chair, with Mordur, happily, back on the armrest again.

Uncle Thordy looked down at Grandpa and shook his head. "You should be in bed, Uncle Thursten. You're in no condition to meet any of the relatives. They said they'd come as soon as the roads were cleared. Of course, I'd rather take you to the doctor."

"No doctors. Just bring me coffee," Grandpa whispered hoarsely, "thick and black as a witch's brew. Only two places to get the best coffee in the world: Gimli and right here at Thordy's. Coffee the way it was meant to be. It'd bring a statue to life."

"How can I argue with someone so wise?" Uncle Thordy went to the kitchen and returned a moment later with the coffee. Grandpa could barely hold it, but he managed to sip without spilling a drop. He glared over the steaming cup. "Stop gawking at me ... you'd think you'd never seen a man drink coffee before."

We sat back. Maybe he *was* starting to feel a bit better.

"So what happened?" Grandpa asked.

Uncle Thordy told him, and the rest of us added our two cents.

Grandpa nodded. "So she's still as testy as ever."

"She claimed someone baited Onni," I said. "With a bag of ... of animal innards. And I saw a similar bag this morning outside my window. And at the old croft house."

"It was a butcher bag," Mordur explained. "I do not know where he found it."

"We better get a head count on our sheep tomorrow, Mordur," Uncle Thordy said. "I have an idea where some of those organs may have come from."

"What do you mean?" I asked.

"They looked fresh," Thordy explained. "They might have been *gathered* tonight."

I didn't even want to think about what that meant. Sarah was kind enough to change the topic. "Did you see much of Gunnvor when you were a kid?" she asked Grandpa.

"A few times. And she looked exactly the same as she does now, the poor woman. It's like she doesn't age — or she was born old." He lowered the cup of coffee, resting it on his knee. "She once came down and gave my father what-for because his goats were bleating too loud."

"Isn't she a little too old for children?" I asked.

"I'm not sure whose son he is," Uncle Thordy said. "Or even where he came from. Maybe she adopted him. Mr. Gunnvor died years ago — before I was born. At least no one's seen him since around that time."

"So how old is she, then?" I asked.

Grandpa exchanged looks with Uncle Thordy, who shrugged. "I'd guess she's in her nineties," Grandpa finally answered, but he sounded uncertain.

"And she gets around like that?" Michael said in disbelief. "She cut through two feet of snow like it was nothing."

"I don't know how she does it," Grandpa said. "I should have asked her though. I need a little of her energy now."

I could have used some too, if only to keep track of my thoughts. One suddenly occurred to me: What did my hair look like? I bit my tongue to keep from laughing at myself.

Uncle Thordy cleared his throat as if he were about to speak. We all looked at him, but he just stared back, then shook his head. His face appeared even more tired and depressed, like someone had let all the air out of him. He stood, went into the kitchen, and returned with the same cheeses we had seen at breakfast and some dried, smoked cod.

I devoured everything I could get my hands on. Michael and Sarah dug in too. Even Mordur took a handful.

"I think I'm starting to like this food," I whispered to Sarah.

"It does grow on you. Maybe we're getting tougher."

"So what was wrong with that boy?" Michael asked.

"Your guess is as good as mine," Grandpa said. "I'd bet he suffers from some sort of mental handicap."

"He was covered with blood, though." I helped myself to a chunk of cheese. "What was that from?"

"Maybe he was attacked by the same thing that attacked you," Grandpa suggested.

"No. He would be …" Mordur crossed his arms, shivered. "A child would be torn in two."

"There has to be a connection," Grandpa said. "Odd that he would show up here on the same night. And naked. How did he make it through all that snow?"

Uncle Thordy cleared his throat again. His face had become stony. "Actually, it would be easy. He … he was in a different form when he walked through the blizzard. His wolf form." Uncle Thordy's voice was solemn, each word said without emotion.

"He what?" Grandpa Thursten asked.

"He's an *úlfr-madr*. A shape-shifter who can become a wolf. Just like the one who killed Kristjanna. That's why he was naked. That's why he's covered with blood. He's the one who attacked you kids at the croft house."

I leaned back into my chair. I didn't like the certainty in Uncle Thordy's voice. I glanced at Grandpa, expecting him to refute this wild claim, but he was wearing his best poker face. He watched Uncle Thordy with curious eyes.

"You think I'm wrong, don't you?" Uncle Thordy accused, jabbing a figure towards Grandpa. "You think it's all in my messed-up head. But you weren't there in that cave. You didn't hold your dead wife in your arms. One of Loki's offspring poked a hole behind her ear and killed her, like it was a game. Maybe it was even little Onni." Uncle Thordy had clenched his hand into a fist and was squeezing so tight it shook. "And now he's got Gunnvor acting as his mother. How do you think she's lived so long? He's shared some of his blood with her. Taken over her mind so she looks after him while he sleeps between kills." Angry red splotches appeared on Uncle Thordy's face. "They don't age like we do. He's probably fifty years old and he looks ten. Who knows where his real parents are."

He lowered his fist, glanced back and forth between all of us. His eyes burned momentarily into mine, daring me to speak out against him. He blinked.

"We all know how much you miss Kristjanna," Grandpa said softly.

Tears began to trickle down Uncle Thordy's cheeks. He gritted his teeth, wiped at his eyes. "Excuse me," he said, quietly. "Forgive me. Forgive me. I am not a good host today." He lifted his bulky body from the chair and trudged down the hall to his room, the scent of his aftershave lingering for a minute. The door closed.

"Uncle Thordy is not feeling well," Grandpa Thursten said, "and I don't know if he'll be better any time soon. It's never easy to get over the death of a loved one."

I remembered standing on the basement stairs at home, watching my father cry so hard that he shook. This was years after Andrew's death. Dad clutched one of Andrew's hockey sweaters in his large hands and cried and cried. I backed slowly up the stairs and left him to his sorrow. Then I went to my own room, closed the door, and bawled into my pillow. Grandpa was right. It wasn't easy to get over the death of someone you loved.

"Grief has been bad to Thordy," Mordur whispered. "My father said when the search party found him they could see big change — he already had ugly bags under his eyes and his hair had turned more gray. Even our dog barked when he came near. Tyr did not know him any more." Mordur hesitated for a moment, then added, "But I am believing Thordy is right."

» 21 «

"Why do you say that?" Grandpa raised his bushy eyebrows.

"Because …" Mordur rubbed at the side of his neck like he was trying to ease a kink "… because my dad once said a story to me. In 1950 a local crofter wounded a female shape-shifter feeding on a reindeer. He caught her in a net and dragged her to the town square at Hvammstangi."

"How did they know she was a shape-shifter?" I asked.

"She had the head and body of a wolf, but she was walking on two legs. She lived only for a few days. They took photographs. I looked it up. There are articles in the library about the strange woman-wolf, even a drawing. People came from every corner of Iceland just to stare at her."

"Did you see the photos?" Sarah asked.

Mordur shook his head. "None were good. Just a shadow lying against the stump of a tree. When she died, her body fell all to pieces. My father went to see her a few hours before that. He said it was the most very frightening thing he had ever laid his eyes on. But he felt sorrow. She was tied to a stake and left to rot while strangers stared. Dad said he had many nightmares after. His mother tried to say it was a circus trick, but he could not believe her. It had looked too real."

"Perhaps he was right," Grandfather said. He coughed another phlegmy cough, then said quietly, "It was my brother Jóhann, Thordy's father, who found that shape-shifter."

We did simultaneous double takes. "What?" I said. "You … you knew about this story?"

Grandfather nodded solemnly. "Yes. My brother phoned and told it to me. I was already living in Manitoba then. He was very excited … I thought he had dreamt up the whole thing. Jóhann had a real gift for exaggerations and he was a little scatterbrained at times. He insisted he had caught a shape-shifter; he even sent me the faded photographs of the lump against the tree. I told him he'd been hoodwinked. Up to his dying day he swore it was a true story. Maybe I shouldn't have doubted him so much." Grandpa coughed again. "There is one thing that bothers me. Jóhann said he could hear a high-pitched howling for weeks afterwards. It sounded like a younger wolf. He believed there was one more."

"Oh great," Michael said, "is it Onni, then?"

Grandfather fell silent, his lips a tight line. He drank from his coffee.

The fire crackled loudly, and I almost jumped out of my seat. I was definitely getting too wound up. No more coffee for me.

"You know, I'd like to see what your father wrote on the calfskins," Grandpa said suddenly. Mordur pulled them out of the wooden box and handed them to Grandpa, who unrolled one and held it up to his face. He squinted, lifted his glasses out of his pocket, and fumbled to put them on. "*Je suis* ... uh, I am ... uh ... It keeps mentioning this name, Skoll, over and over again. And it mentions Kristjanna, too."

"Uncle Thordy's wife?" Michael said. "Why would it mention her?"

Grandpa shrugged. He rubbed at his temple like he was trying to ward off a headache.

"It has the words *loup-garou*," I said. "We thought it might be a story."

"A weird one, if it is." Grandpa had opened the third scroll. "And there's a drawing of the spearhead. It says it's Jón Arason's spear. I wonder if that's Bishop Arason."

"Who?" Sarah asked.

Grandpa wiped some sweat from his forehead. "Bishop Jón Arason was from the sixteenth century. He was sometimes called the last real Icelander because he stuck to his beliefs. In fact he was beheaded by his enemies for those beliefs. He was an historical figure, but, of course, this *is* Iceland — there were folktales about him, too."

"And they had something to do with the spear?" Mordur asked.

"Yes. And an *úlfr-madr*. One of the stories is about a woman whose husband went missing and was later found torn to shreds. They called in the bishop and he told the local blacksmith to forge a spearhead much like the one Einar drew on the calfskin. The bishop dipped the spearhead in holy water and marched into the hills. Hours later, a great howling and screaming was heard. In the morning, Bishop Arason returned with a broken spear. The woman asked him if he had killed the creature and he said, 'Speak of the Devil and you give him life.' In other words, the deed was done, don't give the Devil any more of your time."

"Why would Mordur's dad make the spearhead?" I asked.

"Either it was just a hobby or he believed an *úlfr-madr* was loose. And not just any shape-shifter, but a 'pact-breaker'."

"What do you mean?" Michael lifted up the last piece of cheese and bit into it.

Grandpa squeezed his temples. He was beginning to look even more pale. "Well legend says that around the time Bishop Arason was alive, all of Loki's children made a secret pact with the Icelandic leaders. They promised not to harm another human as long as the shifters were left alone. They took human shapes and lived among us. My father used to tell us tales about the shape-shifters who broke the pact; every hundred years or so, one would give in to the temptation of feeding on human flesh. Like the shifter who attacked him."

Mordur was leaning in, an eager look on his face. "Does the calfskin say more?"

Grandpa stared a bit longer, his eyes scanning the lines, his brow furrowed. "I'm having trouble focusing. Would it … would it be okay if I borrowed these tonight? I — I'd like to take a look at them under better light. Maybe I can tell you something in the morning."

"Oh … yes," Mordur said, a little disappointed. "I will wait."

"I had better go to bed, then," Grandpa said and rubbed his eyes. "Either that or prop my peepers open with tooth-picks."

"Uh …" Sarah began. "Are we going to be safe here?"

"Of course," Grandpa said. "If that boy really is a shape-shifter, he looked to be in no *shape* to return tonight." He paused. A flicker of light came to his eyes. "No shape, to be a shape-shifter. Ha! That's a good one." He wheezed out a laugh as he tried to get up. Sometimes Grandpa was such a goof. I glanced over at Mordur and rolled my eyes in feigned embarrassment. He smiled and nodded. My heart skipped a beat.

Michael gave Grandpa a hand up. "Who knows," Grandpa continued, "in the morning we may wake up and have a good chuckle at all our theories hatched in the mid-dle of the night. *Góda nótt.*"

"Good night," we replied.

"See ya in the morning," Michael said to us as he guided Grandpa to his room.

Sarah looked across at me, then at Mordur. She yawned suddenly — a yawn that looked completely fake — and got up. "Well, I think I'll hit the sack too. Nighty-night." A second later, Mordur and I were alone.

The fire was dying, making the lights on the Christmas tree glow all the brighter. Mordur knelt down, grabbed a poker, and pushed the logs around so the flames grew higher. "This will burn down in a minute. I will stay until then."

"Good," I said, a little too quickly.

Mordur gave me a look. "Good? Why?"

"Uh … well …" I couldn't get my words in any logical order. "I just don't feel sleepy yet."

Mordur hadn't stopped looking at me. "Red hair is good luck."

"What?" I nervously ran my hand through my hair.

"It was a saying my father said. He maybe made it up. He believed every time he met a woman with red hair it was a good-luck day."

"Did he have a thing for redheads?"

Mordur nodded. "Yes. He and I had a lot in common."

It took a while for this to sink in. "So am I good luck to you?"

"We will see," he said. "I have not met too much girls from outside Iceland who know the old myths as well as you."

"How many girls do you know from other countries?"

"Just you." Mordur poked at the logs. Sparks flew up, but the flames were dying. "I wish this all was not happening right now," he said, his voice turning serious. "I wish I knew what my father wrote on those calfskins." He stared grimly at the embers.

"I'm sure Grandpa will figure out your dad's letter," I said softly. "And if he can't, there must be someone in town who can read French."

"I hope so." Mordur didn't sound hopeful. "This day has made me wonder about how my father died. He drowned while fishing. Just another Icelander stolen by the ocean, out trying to earn a couple kroners while work on the farm was slow. But there was something — how do you say? — spooky? — about it. Heim, another fisherman, said he saw a figure rise out of the water and pull my father down into the waves."

"Really? What do you think it was?"

"He said it was like a man, but covered with hair. No one else spotted the thing. They just saw my father standing at the edge of the boat in a stormy sea. Then gone. I thought Heim was making up the story. Heim likes his bottle, he is a great big drunk kind of guy. But now I do not know. Maybe the story was true."

We watched the flames die down until they were just red embers. Mordur poked at the logs again. One broke in half, burned brightly for a moment, then faded. "You know that female shape-shifter? My father spoke me about her just before he went to work on the fishing boat. He said he wanted me to think about the story. When he got back I was to tell him whether I thought it was true."

"Why would he do that?"

"I did not know. I thought he was just having fun, he liked to make the jokes. Now I wonder if it was a test. If I said I believed the shape-shifter was real, he might have spoken me what he was writing about."

Even though I wanted to be wide awake for this time with Mordur, my eyelids wouldn't cooperate. I kept talking, hoping it would keep my energy up. "You know, it's weird, but Grandpa told us that our great-grandfather killed a shape-shifter. Now we find out that Uncle Thordy's dad killed one, too. It's like this valley is cursed."

"It is," Mordur said softly. He got up onto his haunches, felt his side.

"How are your ribs?" I asked.

"Better. Just bruises. Nothing worth complaint." The last ember grew dark. "I should go home." Mordur checked that the chain-link curtain on the fireplace was closed tightly.

I went with him to the porch, flicked on the outside light. His house was only about fifty yards away, visible through a small window. It was calm out now, though it hadn't stopped snowing.

"Will you be all right there? Your place looks so small."

He smirked. "Are you worried for me, Angie?"

"Well ... yes, of course."

He scratched at his temple, like he was thinking real hard. "Does that mean you like me?"

"I ... uh. Well ..." My tongue was tied in triple knots. "I — I don't really know you. But I like you."

He grinned. "I know. And I hope all this bad time goes away, soon. Maybe even tomorrow. You are not here for long. It would be good to talk more. You could speak to me about what it is like to live in America."

"That would be nice." My heart had sped up and butter-flies were fluttering inside my stomach. "Really nice."

"Well, I go. And do not be worried about me." He pulled the spearhead his father had made from his pocket. "This will protect me," he joked. "Good night, Angie."

He walked out into the fresh, thick snow. I watched until he disappeared into his house and the light came on.

» 23 «

I went to my room and threw myself down on top of my cot. "So let me get this straight," I said to Sarah, who was still up, reading. "Mordur's not related to us? He's the son of the hired man? So …"

"So you can kiss him," Sarah finished.

"Hey, wait a minute, that's not what I was figuring out," I said, though it was *exactly* what I was figuring out.

"Well, if you did think that, you wouldn't be alone." She fluffed her hair, acting like some kind of model. "Lucky for you, I'm already taken."

I huffed out a sigh. The coffee was still zigging around my system, and everything else that happened was zagging through my brain. "This has been the weirdest day of my life," I announced. My body was drained. I felt immensely tired and yet I couldn't do much but sit up in bed and stare at the wall, wrapping the comforter tightly around me. I wanted to collapse into sleep, but it was impossible.

Mordur seemed different than any other boy I'd met. Exotic, I guess. I wanted to find out more about him. It must have been hard growing up with his mother living somewhere else and not wanting to spend time with him. And to not have a dad anymore.

"So what do you think it is?" Sarah asked, startling me.

I was so busy daydreaming I'd forgotten she was in the room. It took me a moment to figure out what her question was about. "I don't know," I answered slowly. "Something that's very smart."

"What if I said I believe Uncle Thordy?"

Just a few hours ago I would have called her crazy. But now I simply asked her why.

"Did you see when it was coming up the ladder into the loft? Its head … it was animal-like, but there was something human about it. You said it seemed very smart — smart enough to climb a ladder and lift up a trapdoor. Smart enough to get into the barn and steal a sheep. And the way it moved was unlike anything I'd ever seen. But it wasn't much bigger than that boy. Just very, very strong."

"Onni had a mark near his eye. Almost like he'd been hit with a fire poker."

Sarah nodded. She didn't seem surprised by this information. "Do you remember the story Grandpa told us on the plane?"

"About Great-Grandpa and the bear?"

"Why do you think he told us that story?"

"I don't know. To scare us. To pass the time."

"All good reasons. But he really believed it. He told it with such conviction, like he was seeing it through his father's eyes. I have a theory, Angie. I think we're all connected to our ancestors. We share the same genes, the same dreams, and often the same lives. Think of Grettir the Strong. I've actually had dreams about him. How many battles did he have against evil in his life?"

"He fought a lot of ghosts and things. And people too, don't forget. He was an outlaw."

"Yes, but he's remembered for being a hero. We have ... the essence ... of each of our ancestors somewhere in our muscles, in our minds, and perhaps most importantly in our spirit. And sometimes that stuff just comes out."

"Like when you yelled those Icelandic words back in the croft house?" I said.

"Yes, it was partly what I read, but partly what was passed down to me, like one of our ancestors had been in a situation like that and knew what to say. What do you think?"

I'm about two steps from freaking out, is what I wanted to say. That only two days ago I was safe at home in North Dakota.

Sort of safe. Back at home I'd had the nightmares.

"We *are* connected to our ancestors," I answered. The hair on the back of my neck slowly stood up. I described the dreams I'd had about the wolf.

She listened silently, nodded. "I've had dreams like that too; seeing things before they happened. I once dreamed Michael was going to break his arm on a school trip. I even felt it crack. I convinced him to pretend he was sick and stay home. One of his classmates ended up breaking his arm at a tour of a metal factory. Kind of weird, but so what? So you and I seem to be a little psychic. Does it mean this wolf-thing is real?"

"My gut tells me one thing," I said, "but my brain tells me this is all our imagination." I lay back against my pillow. "There's still something bothering me: the quarrel Mordur and Uncle Thordy had about us going to the croft house. Why did Uncle

Thordy let us go if he believed this creature was out there?"

Sarah sat completely still for a moment, almost like she was meditating. "Do you think we were bait? He's had a year and a half to really learn how to hate this wolf-thing. Maybe he thought he could get rid of it."

"But to risk our lives —"

My words were cut off by the smashing of glass and a fearful cry from Grandpa's room.

» 24 «

Sarah and I sat frozen. Something heavy bashed against the wall, shaking the house. Grandpa yelled again, more a cry of anger than fear this time. Deep, loud growling, all too familiar, floated under our door. Then came the sound of a struggle followed by a sharp yelp.

"Grandpa!" I yelled, running out of the bedroom and down the hall. I pushed my way inside his room, Sarah one step behind me.

The lights were out and it was freezing because the window had been smashed. Glass glittered on the floor, catching moonlight. I couldn't see Grandpa.

Michael charged in, blinking the sleep out of his eyes. "What happened?"

Sarah clicked the light switch. The shade on the ceiling was partially broken, but the bulb flickered with enough light to show that Grandpa was in the corner, crumpled against the wall. I rushed up to him. Something pierced my right heel, but I ignored it. "Grandpa," I whispered, leaning down, touching his cold face.

"Afi," Sarah said from beside me.

He was out cold. His left cheek had two crisscrossing lines of scratches that looked like claw marks. Thankfully they weren't deep. Lying beside him was a small letter opener, blackened by blood. I pointed it out to Sarah. We surveyed the room. The desk was broken, along with the lamp beside it. Shredded paper had been scattered across the floor.

Grandpa opened his eyes. It took a moment for him to recognize us. "I got him," he wheezed. "Loki's offspring is fast, but I got the big beast. Right in the chest." He was clutching one of the calfskin pages. It had been torn almost in half. A chunk had been bitten out of the top.

"Let's move him to the living room," Sarah said. I took one arm, Sarah another, and Michael grabbed his feet. We lifted Grandpa and he felt unnaturally light. We carried him down the hallway and Michael kicked at Uncle Thordy's door as we passed. We didn't pause to see if he was awake. We lay Grandpa on the couch.

He sighed. There were several tears in his pajamas revealing cuts in his skin, but none seemed life-threatening and he'd stopped bleeding. His breath was ragged. Michael pulled a blanket off the back of the couch and we covered him.

"I could only read some of Einar's warning," Grandpa said hoarsely.

It dawned on me that he meant the writing on the calfskin.

"Einar knew. He knew. He said there are two of Loki's children in this valley. One was called Skoll, the Scarred One. The wolf who ate the sun. He liked to kill his victims slowly, by poking one claw behind their ear."

Grandpa gasped suddenly and pressed a hand against his chest. He looked at Sarah and me. "I know what Odin said to Baldur," he whispered. His eyes slid closed.

Sarah put her hand on Grandpa Thursten's arm and shook him gently, but he remained unconscious. "We've got to take him into Hvammstangi, to the hospital. Go get Uncle Thordy."

I went to his room and pounded on the door. "Uncle Thordy, wake up!"

I hit the door again. "Grandpa's been hurt. Wake —"

The door opened on its own. A chilly breeze ran across my skin. I reached around for the light switch, flicked it on. The room stunk like rotten meat, such a strong stench I had to cough. The bed was made. The window was open.

How could he live in such a gross-smelling room?

I ran back to the living room yelling, "He's gone, Uncle Thordy's gone!"

"I'm going to call the police," Michael said. "This is getting too damn weird." He went into the kitchen and scrambled around, looking for a phone book.

I knelt down. My foot was aching. I lifted it, found a dark stain on my sock. A shard of glass stuck out near the heel. I gritted my teeth, pulled out the glass, and tossed it in the garbage. I found tissue in the kitchen and stuck it down my sock to mop up the bleeding. I'd have to do a better job later. I sat beside Grandpa and squeezed his hand. It was cold.

"Who's this Skoll Grandpa was talking about?" I asked Sarah.

"He said Skoll was the wolf who ate the sun. Maybe its the same wolf who appears in the myths during the final battle."

"I dreamed about a wolf eating the sun," I said. "What's that mean?"

"I don't know." Sarah shook her head. "I just don't know at all."

"Well, what did Grandpa mean about knowing what Odin said to Baldur?"

"It was the great secret of the Norse myths. At Baldur's funeral, just before they were going to light the ship on fire, Odin whispered a secret to Baldur, but no one knows what it was."

"Why would Grandpa say that?"

Sarah's eyes were wet. It took her a moment to finally say, "Because he believes he's going to die."

"No," I whispered, tightening my grip on Grandpa's hand, feeling him there, very much there but getting colder and somehow farther away.

» 25 «

"They're going to try and send an ambulance," Michael said as he came into the room. "The *logga* — the police, or whatever they call them — are coming too. *If* they can plow through all that snow. I guess the storm was twice as bad around Hvammstangi. The main highway is blocked."

"What if no one makes it here?" I asked. Grandpa's hand was like ice now. "I don't know much about first aid."

"If Grandpa gets worse, we'll have to phone back and get advice." Michael knelt down next to the couch. "The woman on the phone said it's just important to keep him warm."

Sarah had her palm on Grandpa's forehead. Grandpa's eyes were closed, his face solemn. "He doesn't seem to be waking up. He has a heck of a fever, but at least he's breathing. That's a good sign."

"What if he's in a coma?" I asked. I tucked Grandpa's

hand under the blanket, then went to the end of the couch and covered his feet. "What are we going to do?"

"What can we do?" Michael asked. "Should I look for Uncle Thordy?"

"Go outside?" Sarah shook her head. "We don't know what's out there. We're safest right where we are."

"What about Mordur?" I said. "We can't just leave him alone."

I went to the kitchen window, scraped at the ice, and peeped through the clear spot. "The light's still on, so I guess he's awake," I said on my way back to the living room.

"We could phone him," Sarah suggested.

"He doesn't have a phone, remember?" I said.

Michael stood, his hands balled up into fists like he was gearing up for a fight. "Someone will have to go over there. But one of us has to look after Grandpa."

"How do we decide who stays?" Sarah asked.

"Rock, paper, scissors," I said. It was a hand game we'd played since we were kids, often using it to decide who would ask our parents for extra ice-cream money. We held out our hands. Mine was shaking slightly, even though I tried to hold it still. "On the count of three, loser stays."

Sarah counted aloud. On three, both Michael and I put our hands out flat, meaning we chose paper. Sarah made a fist.

"Paper covers stone," Michael said. "I guess you'll have to stay, sis."

"We don't have time for a best out of three, do we?" she asked. She hugged both of us quickly. "For good luck," she explained. "Now hurry back."

We threw on our winter clothes and jammed our feet into our boots. I went back to the kitchen and found a large flashlight in the cupboard, heavy enough that it could be used as a weapon.

Sarah had pulled a chair up beside Grandpa and was holding one of his hands in both of hers, concentrating as if she were praying. She didn't look up as I passed her.

Michael grabbed the axe from inside the closet and hefted it in his hands. "Let's go," he said and we stepped out into the open. It was still snowing lightly, but the air was calm. Despite that, we had a tough time slogging through the snowbanks, sinking up to our knees and higher. The tires on Uncle Thordy's vehicle were completely buried, and they were *big* tires. I had a sick feeling that it would be ages before an ambulance or cops got here. We were too far from town, and if the roads were clogged up anything like Uncle Thordy's driveway, they'd be completely impassable.

The moonlight seemed to be growing dimmer and dimmer, as if somewhere in the heavens something was taking bites out of it. I thought of the wolf who chased the moon through the sky. Too many of my dreams were becoming reality.

Mordur's outside light served as our guiding beacon. When we got to the house we discovered the door partly open, a small bank of snow already building up against it. The light from inside the house revealed tracks that were quickly being filled in.

I yanked on the door and it got jammed in the snow, but there was just enough room to stumble inside. "Mordur!" I shouted. What I saw pulled me up short. A pitcher had been shattered on the floor, shards of glass scattered across the tile. The table was knocked over, along with a stack of books. One wall was a bookshelf, more books were lying beside it. "Mordur!" I cried, running into the bedroom. I flicked on a light switch but nothing happened. I pointed my flashlight around, saw an unmade bed. The tiny room was empty.

Michael stood in the doorway of the bathroom. "He's gone," he said, kneeling down next to what looked like a broomstick. "But he didn't go without a fight." The stick was actually a handle that could have come from a pitchfork. Clamped at one end was the four-edged spearhead. A book was open beside it, full of illustrations.

"It looks like Mordur was doing some research," Michael said, lifting up one of the books. I glanced back at the spear. Next to it was a pool of blood.

"He's been hurt!" I said. I looked closer. Streaks of blood led to the door.

"I'm not sure what to do." Michael's face was pale. "I don't think we can take that thing on."

"Maybe it's weaker now. Grandpa wounded it. And Mordur might have, too. Maybe this isn't his blood. It —"

A low moan came from just outside the open door. Someone was crawling in the snow, trying to get in the house.

"Do you see that?" Michael whispered. He gripped the axe with both hands.

I bent down slowly, slipped my hand around the shaft of the spear, and lifted it, feeling its weight, light and balanced like it would strike a straight blow. We stayed still.

There was another moan and a man lifted his head, trying to look into the house. *"Help,"* a soft voice said. *"Help me."*

His hand grasped the bottom of the door, pulled it open further.

It was Mordur, crawling through the snow, trying to squeeze himself inside. His face was bruised, a cut bled on his forehead. His eyes swiveled in their sockets like he was trying to focus. He looked right at me and pushed his hand out towards me.

I moved to help him, lowering the spear, but Michael grabbed my shoulder. "Wait! I see something else."

A tall shadow was visible just outside the door, a figure slightly hunched over. It had a grip on Mordur's leg.

"Help me … get inside," Mordur whispered. "The shifter is right here."

I raised the spear, Michael brought his axe up, and without any signal from the other, we charged ahead. The shape was becoming clearer. And larger.

Just as we got to the door, the creature jumped back. It kept a tight hold on Mordur, dragging him out into the deep snow, like it was playing a game with us. It crouched over Mordur. Its long, muscled back was covered with matted hair. Tattered clothing hung from its body. Its red eyes glared at us over a long snout. In a heartbeat I knew that our worst nightmare was true.

Another shape-shifter, larger than the last, stood just feet away.

Compared to the one that had attacked us at the croft house this one seemed full grown.

"Skoll," I whispered.

It seemed to nod when I said its name. We stepped towards the beast and it jumped up and thrust its arm into the air.

The light over the door burst, showering us with glass and electric sparks.

» 26 «

We lifted our hands to guard our eyes. In that moment the shape-shifter had begun running from us, dragging Mordur by the feet like he was a rag doll. "There!" I pointed. They were a good ten yards away already. Mordur called to us, lashing out with his arms, trying to get a grip on something and pull himself free. His head bounced through the snowbanks.

Michael and I ran after them, sinking into the snow. We passed the barn and headed towards the plateau. The further we went, the deeper the snow got, but we were able to keep them in our sight for a little while at least. Mordur made one more cry for help, then they disappeared over a rise. All we were left with were tracks.

I flicked on my flashlight, carrying it in one hand, the spear still in the other. Here and there, splashes of blood stained the snow.

"That better not be Mordur's blood," I said.

"I just hope he's still alive when we find him," Michael said, gripping the axe with both hands, looking like some kind of insane tree cutter. "Did you see how huge that thing was?"

"It's Skoll. The one mentioned in the calfskins."

"I was beginning to figure that out," Michael said. "But I was hoping I was wrong."

We ran as fast as we could, following the beam of my flashlight. I wasn't exactly sure of our direction, but it seemed we were climbing a hill heading towards the grazing fields. I turned back and the lights of Uncle Thordy's house shone like distant stars.

A few steps later, we lost the footprints. They just stopped, like the shifter had vanished. I pointed the flashlight in a wide arc, but all the snow ahead of us was untouched.

"Where did they go?" Michael was huffing, sweat glistening on his face. Steam rose from his skin, looking ghostly in the moonlight. We headed blindly into the open snow.

The sound of Mordur screaming stopped us in our tracks. We listened, trying to pinpoint the direction.

"Up there." Michael pointed to a rock wall barely visible a short distance away. It was about six feet high. "It's coming from up there."

We cut through the snow, climbed the wall. At the top, the land was flat again. The flashlight revealed a gray patch of cloth hanging from the branch of a small bush. A sickening feeling came over me.

"It's part of Mordur's sweater," I said, pulling the tattered rag off. I held it in the same hand as the spear. "He's probably freezing to death. He …"

"He'll be all right," Michael said. "If that thing wanted to kill him, it would have done it right away. For some reason he's keeping Mordur alive."

Clouds had cleared away from the moon. Rocks and snow were outlined in a cold, blue light. "The tracks start again up there," Michael said, pointing. Then he turned to look back. "I want to know how that thing got from there to here, while carrying Mordur. Did it jump?"

Another cry came from the distance. Like Mordur was in pain.

"Let's go," I said, aiming the flashlight ahead. We dashed on, following the tracks until they took a sharp turn.

"Wait!" I yelled, holding up my hand. "Don't take another step!"

Michael stopped. "What is it?" I pointed the flashlight down. There, just in front of us, was a huge chasm.

"I didn't realize we were getting up so high," Michael said.

I looked over the edge. One more step and we both would have ended up down there, our bones broken, the snow slowly smothering us. My knees felt suddenly weak.

I edged back. Sucked in a deep breath.

"You okay?" Michael had his hand on my back. "Can't you breathe?"

"I'm … fine. We've got to keep going. I just won't look down anymore."

I turned, continued on, following the tracks. We struggled through the snow, across an area littered with large stones. It was like a giant had been bashing at the side of the mountain and this was where the chunks had landed.

We crawled up an embankment. I had to go one-handed, my other hand clutching the spear, the flashlight stuffed in my coat pocket. It would have been near impossible for the shifter to drag Mordur up here. It was at least six feet straight up, but at the top we found the marks again. A piece of

Mordur's sweater was torn and hanging from some rocks.

"The shifter is leaving this trail on purpose," I said. "He wants to be sure we don't get lost."

Michael's face looked pale and cold in the light of the flashlight. "You're right. But what can we do? We have to try and rescue Mordur."

We kept on going. It wasn't until we had climbed the next rise that we stopped and stared, frozen in our tracks.

A stone house stood across from us. It was built into the side of a mountain. The roof sloped down from high above, stopping near the ground. Just below the roofline, candles flickered in the windows. It was probably one of the oldest stone homes in Iceland, ten times older than anything I'd seen in North Dakota.

I knew it was Gunnvor's.

» 27 «

The footprints and drag marks led to a small barn that sat off to one side of the house, across a snow-covered pasture. I turned and looked down the way we'd come. Two tiny lights were all I could see of Uncle Thordy's farm.

"We better keep quiet," Michael said, looking around, the axe in his hand.

"And out of sight," I added, switching off the flashlight. The moon cast a silvery glint over everything. Michael led. I followed silently behind him, keeping a good, strong grip on the spear.

The barn seemed even older than Uncle Thordy's, a low, flat building with a door in the center, barely big enough to fit a horse through. One side of the building was partially collapsed. We passed through a broken wooden fence and stopped. The barn shifted, making it creak like it was on the edge of collapse.

"The tracks go in here," Michael said and slowly pulled the door open. We stood back for a moment, not wanting to enter the pitch blackness. I flicked on the flashlight, checked as far as I could see, and took the first step inside.

The place was empty. I took another cautious step and Michael followed me in.

The air smelled old, musty. The straw on the floor had turned gray with age. I swept the flashlight around, lighting up different corners of the barn. A large roof beam had collapsed, so the ceiling at the far side of the barn sagged nearly to the floor. The remains of a stall stuck out of one wall. At one time it might have held a cow, but there was no sign of any animals anymore.

Nothing had been kept in here for years. I swung the light around again. My cheeks tingled and I worried it might be frostbite.

"Where is he?" Michael whispered.

Then my light caught a gray cloth lying in the far corner. "Michael, what's that?"

We ran to it, ducking under the roof beam. It was another piece of Mordur's sweater. Beside it, opened like someone had been interrupted having lunch, were three cloth bags, each bursting with livers and hearts, laid out like a sacrifice.

"Do they ever stink," Michael said, holding his hand over his nose. "You could smell them from a mile away."

"Uhhhn," someone moaned. "Whazzhapp — "

Above us, the beams creaked. Slowly we raised our heads.

» 28 «

Before I could point my flashlight up, a black shape landed with a thud on Michael, forcing him to his knees, then face first to the floor. The axe flew from his hand. I screamed and dropped the flashlight.

"Get it off me!" Michael yelled, desperately struggling with his attacker. I grabbed the flashlight, pointed it, only to see it wasn't a wolf, but a man. A man in a tattered gray sweater. Michael thrust with all his limbs, flipping the man over. He landed on his back, where he lay, still silent. Michael scrambled away, climbed to his feet.

We crept toward the body and I shone my light in its face.

Mordur.

His face was deathly pale, his cheeks scratched. His eyes flickered open for a moment. "Uhhhn," he moaned again, then shut his eyes.

"He just fell on me," Michael said. "Or he was pushed."

I quickly flashed the light around the barn again and up into the rafters. No one was waiting there for us. "Skoll's gone," I said. "He must have left before we got here."

Mordur had a gash on his forehead, but the blood was dry. I knelt and put my hand on his neck. It was warm, his pulse strong. I breathed a sigh of relief. At least he wasn't dead. Not yet, anyway.

"Mordur," I said and gently pulled up one of his eyelids with my thumb. I shone the light into his eye. It was rolled back in its socket. "Wake up, Mordur."

Mordur's clothes were ripped all over, right down to his skin. His sweater had huge chunks out of it, showing his white undershirt.

"Take a look behind his ear," Michael said urgently and knelt down next to me.

We tilted Mordur's head, pulled back an ear. I wiped away a patch of dried blood and found a circular wound about the width of my little finger.

"It looks like a puncture," Michael said. "Just like …"

"… what killed Uncle Thordy's wife," I finished. My hands were trembling now. Only a short time ago Mordur and I had been sitting by the fire, talking. Now he might not ever talk again. I checked his eyes again, but there was no change. "Wake up," I whispered, "Wake up, Mordur. I'm right here." I shook him.

"Angie." Michael put his hand on my shoulder. "I don't think that's going to work."

I examined the wound again. It looked familiar. It suddenly dawned on me that it was just like the one in Grandpa's back. Is that what had been making him so sick? But if it was a similar wound, then how had Grandpa gotten it? My heart began beating even faster.

"We've got to get out of here," I said. I lifted under one of Mordur's shoulders, testing his weight.

"It's a long way home. It'll be tough to carry him back the way we came."

"What else can we do?" I asked.

"I don't know ... we need something ... a sled ..."

"Why don't you build a snowmobile while you're at it?"

"Don't get snarky, I'm just trying to help."

I huffed out a breath of air. "Sorry, we ... we just don't have time to build a sled."

"Why do you think it stuffed Mordur up there?" Michael asked.

"I don't know."

"Maybe it was like a good place to store its ... uh ... food. Like a meat locker. Maybe Uncle Thordy's in these rafters somewhere, too." Michael peered up. I pointed the flashlight, revealing thick cobwebs littered with dust.

I shone the light back on the butcher's bags. "They're bait, aren't they? And the way Mordur was dragged here and stuffed in the rafters, almost like he was ..."

"Bait," Michael finished. "It's like Skoll has set a trap."

29

"We'd better go," I said. "C'mon, help me."

I shoved the flashlight in my pocket and grabbed underneath one of Mordur's shoulders, still holding the spear tight with my left hand. Michael got a hold of Mordur's other shoulder and we dragged him ahead. The door had swung partly closed.

"Did you hear that?" Michael asked.

"What?"

We stood still, listening. I couldn't see anything through the slats on the door. I opened my mouth to say something, then I heard a noise — a soft padding sound and sniffing, just outside the door. It shook gently.

"Well, this is just great," Michael said, letting go of Mordur and tightly gripping the axe.

As I lowered Mordur, his eyes flickered open, then he passed out again. I pointed the spear in front of me, my hands shaking. At least I had a weapon. One made by Mordur's father, just to hunt these wolves. These shifters. All I had to do was get one good blow.

The door rattled suddenly.

Michael and I backed up beside each other, guarding Mordur. There were two dim lights just beyond the door, flickering. Or were they blinking eyes?

"Do you see it?" Michael asked.

"No."

"It's there, crouched down just outside the door … waiting."

He had better vision than me. I stared at the same place, could only see a shadow within a shadow. A low growl sounded through the flimsy slats of the door, grew until it hit a howling crescendo.

The door burst open.

I brought the spear up, bracing myself for the impact.

30

There was nothing there, as if all that noise and force had come from a great gust of wind. We held our positions for a few moments, my muscles growing tight.

I lowered the tip of the spear and just then a gray blur flew through the door. It struck with the force of a cannon-ball, knocking us across the floor. We screamed out in terror. I dropped the spear as my face was ground across the rocky floor, getting a mouthful of old straw. I smashed my head against the wall and rolled into a ball. A snarl echoed all around me.

"Stay back!" Michael hollered. "Get away!" His axe rung off the stone floor, sparks flying everywhere.

The beast got louder and louder, a vicious sound that reverberated through the whole barn, threatening to bring the timbers down around us. Then it dived. Michael groaned, dropping the axe. He was being attacked by something that was actually smaller than him. Onni, I thought. It looks like Onni. The shifter had clamped its jaws into his arm and was shaking its head back and forth, banging him around, playing with him like he was a toy. Michael groaned in pain.

My cousin was being murdered. I staggered to my feet yelling, "Onni! Get away! Leave him alone!" My voice was not my own. It was thick and loud.

Something snapped in front of my face. Teeth. Big, yellow, bloodied teeth. In the blink of an eye Onni had crossed half the length of the barn. He raised a hand and bashed me to the floor, then grabbed my leg, jarring my ankle.

I tried to scramble away, but his grip was too tight. I jammed my hand in my jacket pocket, came out with the flashlight, flicked it on.

Onni squinted into the beam of light. Slaver dripped from his jaws, eyes glowing. Even with the snout-shaped face, I recognized him. A little boy in wolf's clothing, his breath hot and reeking of decay. Ragged, rotten pieces of meat caught between his teeth.

There was a grunting noise behind him. Michael swung the axe, striking Onni on the side of the head with a heavy thump. Onni slowly turned, unaffected by the blow. Michael looked at the axe, realized he'd hit Onni with the blunt end.

Onni let go of me, rose up on his haunches. Michael pulled back for another swing and Onni head-butted him, knocking him backwards.

I sat up. My flashlight had fallen to the ground, the light shining towards the spear. I grabbed the shaft, used it to help me get off the ground. My vision was jumbled, gray and black shapes swirled around. Onni had his back to me. I began running, spear out, balanced easily in my hand as if I had done this a hundred times before. Just as I reached him, ready to thrust the spear, Onni spun around, arms wide. He leapt. I raised the spear, caught him in mid-air near the side of his chest. A bluish light exploded from his flesh as he shrieked. The end of the shaft dug into the floor and the weight of his body snapped the shaft just below the spearhead. Onni fell, his sharp claws just brushing the side of my face, carving out five tiny lines of pain.

He clutched his side, howling, and twisted around, the spearhead embedded in his chest. He kept scratching at it, trying to pull it out. Sparks of light shot up and down what was left of the shaft.

Then he let out one last desperate howl.

It was answered by another long, mournful howl. Outside, and getting closer.

» 31 «

"We can't beat the larger one," Michael said. We stood, unarmed, staring through the door, out into the night. The howling outside grew louder.

"Are you all right?" I asked.

"I think my arm's broken. And I cut my back. How about you?"

"I should be hurting everywhere, but I just feel numb."

Onni was now writhing around and whimpering in front of us. Moonlight flooded through the broken door, outlining him with silver. Bubbles of saliva frothed at his mouth and he opened and closed his jaws like a fish out of water. His hands were still clasped around the shaft of the spear, but he couldn't budge it. The occasional spark appeared in his wound, making him wince.

A shadow fell across him. A hulking figure stood there, eyes glowing red. Skoll had returned.

"Simple-minded humans." The voice was so hoarse it took me a moment to understand the words. "Know nothing, understand nothing. You never change."

The shadow took another step, eyes not moving from us. Skoll's face was in shadows. He stepped into the barn.

The moonlight revealed long, gray, shoulder-length hair. And female features.

"It's Gunnvor," I whispered, shocked.

There was an odd look to her face, like it had been pulled forward and stretched. It was coated with thick hair. Her open mouth revealed long, sharp teeth behind thick lips. She knelt, placed her hand on Onni's forehead and he turned to her. "He's just a child." Her words were still hoarse, but somehow softer. "He doesn't know any better. He can't control himself."

"He was trying to kill us," Michael said.

"You are on our land," Gunnvor said, matter-of-factly. "We have been here much longer than any of you interlopers. And now you come right to my home and attack my child. We should have slain you all years ago."

"We didn't want to come here," I pleaded. "He dragged one of our friends up here."

Her eyes moved from me to Mordur. "Ah, Mordur. Thordy's little helper. Onni didn't touch him." She paused. Sniffed. Looked over at the bags of internal organs. "Lamb livers. Chicken hearts. You wanted to lure my son here and kill him with your little weapon."

"Those were already here," Michael said.

Gunnvor ignored him and bent down and scooped up her son like he was a baby. He had changed slightly; his hair had shortened, making his face look younger but still wolf-like. Without giving him any warning she yanked out the spearhead. He shrieked.

Gunnvor threw the spear down so that it dug into the stone floor. Sparks arced through the air. "You came to murder my child. It has been four hundred years since I last killed one of your kind, but I will not hesitate to start again tonight." She gently set Onni down in a pile of old straw. He reached out to her, but she turned and stepped toward us.

» 32 «

I didn't move. Neither did Michael. There was no point in fighting. We had no spear. No strength. I straightened my spine and faced her. At least she'd see we came from a strong line of Icelanders.

Gunnvor was changing before our eyes. Five long claws grew out of her right hand. She raised it up slowly to strike us. Then she stopped, sniffed deeply, and sniffed again. She dropped her hand, pushed us apart, and strode by. "One of our kind," she hissed, "one of our kind is behind this." She ran from corner to corner, howling and growling, knocking against timbers so the whole building shook.

"Get out! Get out!" she yelled. "Stupid children. You bring bad luck. Little evil creatures. Get off our land. I'll find your master and kill him."

She picked up Onni, backed out of the doorway, and tramped through the thick snow towards her home. I let out a gasp. My body had been wound tight as a knot. The adrenaline in my system grew thinner. My head began to ache and my ankle tingled with pain.

"What was she talking about?" I asked.

"I don't know, but I don't want to stick around and quiz her." Michael rushed over to Mordur. I paused to pull the spearhead out of the floor. There was only a handful of the shaft attached to the point. It took a bit of a tug to get it out. I stuffed it in one of my padded pockets.

We tried to revive Mordur, whispering his name and gently slapping his face. I felt his forehead and it was burning with fever. We lifted him under his shoulders and dragged him out of the barn and into the snow. Step by step, we plodded along. My ankle was starting to throb and I found it hard to put weight on it. I glanced towards Gunnvor's house and thought I could see someone in the window.

"Hurry," I whispered. We pulled Mordur down to the edge of the plateau. The air was chilly and clear.

"The lights look miles away," Michael said, pointing at some glowing dots far below us.

I was so tired. Michael climbed to the bottom of a short rock wall. Between the two of us, we were barely able to lower Mordur down. Michael slipped and Mordur was jarred out of our grip, landing with his face partially buried by snow. We hurried over, pulled him out. I brushed snow off his cheeks.

"Sleeping Beauty didn't feel a thing," Michael said. "You need a rest yet?"

I answered by grabbing Mordur's shoulder and pulling. Michael joined me and we continued on. My ankle was getting worse, and Mordur was growing heavier, as if with every step his bones and flesh were turning to stone. For a time we were able to drag him easily thanks to the slope of the plateau.

At the bottom of the path that had taken us to Gunnvor's was another cliff wall, a drop of some six feet, too far to lower Mordur. We pulled Mordur along it for what seemed hours, but couldn't find an easy way down. Finally, we gave up and collapsed with Mordur lying between us, looking like he was having a lovely sleep. For an absurd moment I thought it was funny.

"I can't go any farther," I admitted, "not without a good rest."

"Me either. We must be off her land by now — she won't chase us here will she?"

"I don't know, but we'll never be able to get Mordur home on our own. My ankle's sprained. We need help."

"Well, we can just wait, someone's got to be looking for us by now. They'll see our tracks."

"What if they don't? We can't just leave Mordur here." I looked around. There was an overhang of rock that would protect us. "Help me move him over there; it should be warmer. You'll have to go home and bring some help. Maybe the police have arrived. Uncle Thordy probably has a sled or a toboggan we could use."

"I can't just leave you here."

"It makes the most sense. You're the one who's still got two good legs. Just help me move him."

It seemed to take forever. We finally pushed Mordur into the corner. "Now go," I said. "You can get help. Go!"

Michael gave me a quick hug, guarding his sore arm. "I'll come back soon, I promise."

I watched him disappear into the distance.

I sat cradling Mordur's head on my lap. Carrying Mordur down the cliff had taken everything I had. Now that we'd stopped moving, I could tell how much I had sweated. Perspiration had gathered on my back, soaked my clothes, and was turning into ice. I began to shiver. I hugged myself to warm up, but it wasn't enough. I kept moving my fingers in their gloves and my toes in their boots. As long as I could wiggle them, I figured they weren't frostbitten.

I worked at keeping my eyes open. I'd heard stories about a group of cross-country skiers back home who'd gotten lost. They finally sighted the ski lodge, but sat down to rest and drifted off to sleep, convinced they would wake up soon and ski the rest of the way. Instead, covered by a blanket of snow, they froze to death.

The moon was high in the sky. Stars flickered and blinked. I felt small, staring up at lights that had been moving in their own secret ways and patterns for millions of years.

Then — for a moment I thought I was hallucinating — I heard a male voice say, "Michael must be long gone now."

I sat straight up. Where had it come from?

"What? Who's there?" I grabbed at a chunk of rock to use as a weapon, but it was frozen to the ground.

"Don't be frightened, it's just me." A figure appeared from around the edge of the alcove. At first all I saw were two legs in torn pants. Then he knelt down and a bearded face, darkened by shadow, looked in. He was smiling.

"Uncle Thordy!" I cried out, relieved. A wave of joy swept over me. "You've found us."

He laughed. "It wasn't hard; you left a well-marked trail."

"But what happened to you? How did —" I took a good look at his clothing. It was torn into rags and he was bleeding from his side. "You're hurt."

This made him chuckle again. "It's nothing. It's healing as we speak. Soon the wound will be closed."

I didn't know what he meant. His eyes were a little glazed

over. Perhaps he was in shock. "Uncle Thordy," I said, "we need to get Mordur back home before we freeze to death. Are you well enough to help me?"

"Oh, no. It is *you* who will help me," he replied, a lightness in his voice like he was saying something funny. "Everything is working out fine."

"Fine? What's that mean?"

"I was waiting. Letting you two take care of the wolf boy. I was hoping you'd kill him, but wounding him was enough."

"What are you talking about? Why would you want us to go up there?"

Uncle Thordy moved ahead so the moonlight fell directly on his face. His eyes were luminous, like they were lit from inside his head.

"Uncle Thordy, what do you mean —"

"Oh, be quiet!" he snapped. "You and your repulsive little family will be rotting in hell soon enough."

I backed away from him, up against the wall. He *had* gone crazy. Or had I? His eyes were glowing now, getting brighter and narrower by the moment.

"Sorry," he said, softly, "it has been a trying time. But don't worry, it'll all be over for you in moments."

His words were icy. My heart sped up. "What do you mean?"

"I mean this." He grinned. His face changed in the light, grew elongated, morphing into a snout. He bared sharp teeth. "Gunnvor's little brat was eating *my* meat. Slaughtering *my* animals. You see, the Onni runt had been hunting on my land. The plateau is where *I* feed, where *my* father fed. That is, before your great-grandfather killed him. We shifters won't spill the blood of another of our kind. It's a pact we made, many years ago, to preserve our race. There are only twenty of us left. But I was quite happy to arrange for you to kill one."

"But·... but you're my ... you're Uncle Thordy how —"

He was changing even more, hair sprouting out of the holes in his clothing. A sick, dead-meat smell wafted through my nostrils. The same smell I'd encountered in Uncle Thordy's house, only stronger.

"Thordy's dead. He died the same day as his wife. His bones are still up there, jammed into a crevice. Only ravens have found them. I assumed his shape, his croft, his life, his name. I have waited a long time to get my hands on your family. To murder two birds with one stone, as you people say."

I was stunned. "You're Skoll," I said, barely able to think. "You carried Mordur up there, didn't you? You left the butcher bags."

"Yes," he admitted, "they have a very distinct smell. Irresistible to a young shape-shifter."

"But, Gunnvor's son, he's not dead. And she's not going to go away. You failed."

"No," Skoll whispered, "not after I'm done with you. I'll limp down to the farm and tell them that Gunnvor herself came and tore you limb from limb. Michael and Sarah will believe me and your grandfather is dead, so he won't be any trouble."

The words hit me like a hammer blow. "What? You're lying."

"Oh, yes, quite dead. He fought off my little pinprick for an amazingly long time. I was impressed. And he was good with an axe, too." He touched the wound at his side.

"*You* attacked him?" I said, feeling an anger spread through my veins. "You?"

"Yes," Skoll said, hissing in my face. "He would have read

all the calfskins. He would have known my little secret. I had to stop him. But let's not dwell on the past. Let me tell you what will happen next. I will kill you. Others in these parts are superstitious enough they'll band together and hunt Gunnvor and the runt down. Then this will be my hunting ground again. As for Mordur, who I dragged so far, he's of no use to me now." Skoll struck Mordur in the chest and Mordur exhaled sharply. He didn't breathe in again. "I can always find another hired man. He was as snoopy and headstrong as his father; I would have had to get rid of him soon enough."

"You smell more like yourself now," a voice said out of the darkness.

Skoll jerked his head up; the look of conceit and pride flashed from his face.

A figure appeared from around the corner, covered in hair, eyes blazing with anger. "Tried to hide your stink with perfume. Stealing the form of a human," Gunnvor accused. "You always were a pact-breaker, just like your father. The circle of elders knows about you now. About your plans. You wanted me and my child dead. We'll feed your liver to our children, that's what we'll do."

Skoll narrowed his eyes, his body shifting shape by the second. "I won't fail," he growled, then threw himself at her. Gunnvor was knocked back into the snow.

I couldn't move. I watched as they battled in the moonlight, exchanging blows. Gunnvor dodged a lunge, swiped her claws across his chest, and Skoll screamed with all his might. But he was larger than her, more powerful, and, even with his wounds, I could see he was winning.

Finally, with a great effort, he lifted Gunnvor and threw her to the ground. She landed on a boulder, her bones cracking like old branches. She lay motionless.

Skoll turned to me. "Now you," he said, wiping blood from his face with a hairy hand. "Now you."

He took a step and his leg gave out. He fell, then tried to stand. Again he fell. He pulled himself up again, moved towards me with a limp.

Finally I had the presence of mind to jump up. I took one last look at Mordur's body, then I began to run, not even sure where, my feet pounding through the snow. My ankle ached, but I ignored it. Skoll's laughter echoed behind me, a long, growling guffaw that turned to a howl.

I kept going, leaping crevice after crevice and charging along narrow paths. I barely kept my footing, winding my way down to another plateau. I couldn't see him, but I could hear him, barking angrily somewhere in the distance.

My eyes were drawn to a falling star burning through the night sky, and for a moment it seemed the heavens were splitting apart.

A light flashed again, this time just ahead of me. Maybe it was a flashlight. Or a snowmobile. I veered towards it.

My lungs were burning, my body drained of energy. Every second step I stumbled.

The light flashed once more, just over a rise in the snow. Was it a trick of the eye. Or was it Skoll's trickery?

It was getting closer now. I ran toward it, hoping for rescuers. Suddenly, the solid ground disappeared from beneath my feet and I fell, landing on soft snow. My breath was knocked from my chest, and my heart stopped beating for a moment. My ears filled with silence. I was lying on my stomach; my muscles refused to obey my commands. Skoll would find me here. An easy victim, even with his wounds.

I tried to breathe deeply, to stand up.

Suddenly I sensed something else in the crevice with

me. Something moving around.

He was here, ready to pounce.

I slowly, ever so slowly, turned my head. There, only a few feet away, was a glimmering form. Familiar, loving eyes looked down on me. A warm smile.

I reached out my hand, whispering, "Hello, Afi."

» 34 «

Grandpa Thursten was alive. Skoll had lied. Grandpa was alive!

He grinned at me, saying, "*Wake up, Sleepyhead. You're not finished yet.*" The cliff walls were visible through him. Stars glistened around his skin. He was dressed in his favorite sweater and tan pants.

"Whaaat?" I asked.

He drifted closer, smoothly, as if there were no snowbanks between us. His feet were bare. I still couldn't find the strength to get up.

But that was okay. Grandpa was here to save me.

He spoke again, his words sounding as if they were coming from a great distance. "*I'm not gone. Not yet. Guess I still have some things to do. So do you, Angie.*"

"Grandpa, I can't move."

"*Angela Laxness, stop lying around.*" The voice was soft, but getting clearer. *"Wake up inside."* He gestured towards the sky. *"You tell her then … she's not listening to me. It's the red hair that makes her that way. She's your sister, maybe she'll listen to you."*

A second, smaller glowing form appeared beside him, floated towards me. As it came closer I recognized his face.

"Andrew," I whispered. He looked the same as he had years ago.

He smiled a mischievous smile and, without a word, leaned down towards me, extending his hand. It was smooth, ivory skinned, and yet through it I could see the stars in the sky. He touched me in the center of my back and I felt a warmth spread up and down my spine. For a moment my mind held an image of Andrew, when we were young, running through the front-yard sprinkler on a hot summer day.

"You're a good big sister," he said. *"You always were."*

I was able to roll over and sit up. I stared at him, wanting to take in as much as I could. Tears began to well up in my eyes.

"Hug Mom and Dad for me." Andrew faded slowly, waving at me.

Grandpa came closer. *"I don't have much time here."* He pointed over a short wall of rocks. *"Go that way. You'll find safety. Get up, lazybones."*

I pushed myself slowly to my feet. Grandpa was growing dimmer. His bare feet were in the snow, but he left no impression.

"Grandpa, what do I do?"

"I don't know. I'm not meant to know. I can hear your grandmother." He paused. *"I've missed her for too many years. It's my time to be with her."*

He was fading.

"Where are you going?"

"No one gave me a travel guide. I'd love to stay around and haunt some more." He laughed, lightly. He sounded like a voice at the end of a long valley. Far away from me. *"I've got to go, Angie. Bless."*

"Afi," I whispered, the tears coming freely now.

He blinked out like a light, like he'd never been there. I stumbled towards where he had been standing, my hands out like a sleepwalker. The air felt warmer for a moment, then it grew chill. "Not yet," I whispered. "Don't go yet."

I lowered my arms. He was gone.

The sound of howling grew louder. Skoll was charging down the hill behind me. I ran in the direction Grandpa had pointed, scrambling to the top of a steep incline.

There, leaning against the side of a mountain and glowing in the moonlight, was the church we had seen the day before.

» 35 «

There wasn't much to the church — a tiny building, maybe three times my height, with two small windows and a door latched by a flat piece of metal. I twisted it and pushed, but it wouldn't budge. When was the last time anyone had been in here?

I threw my shoulder into it. Then, feeling eyes on me, I turned to find Skoll standing just a few yards away.

"Too late, Angie," he rasped, moving slowly towards me. He was holding his side. "Too late for you."

With a final desperate shove, I banged into the door and it swung open so quickly I nearly fell over. I slammed it shut and snapped the latch down and ran into the center of the room. A large stained-glass window at the back of the church let in a dim band of light. I backed down the aisle between two short rows of wooden benches. Dust clogged my nostrils. Something brushed my neck and I almost screamed as I slapped at it. My hand discovered thick spiderwebs, caked with dust and insect wings. I was flicking the sticky mess off my fingers when the door rattled.

Grandpa had said it was safe here. I hoped that meant Skoll couldn't enter this holy place. Maybe there were invisible walls holding him out.

"You can't hide," he yelled. The latch snapped and the door swung open, almost off its hinges. He stood motionless for a moment, his glowing eyes scanning the room until they spotted me. "Why don't you just make this easy on yourself?"

"You … you can't come in here, Skoll. Go on. Go away." I tried to remember the Icelandic words that Sarah had used, but they wouldn't come back to me.

He stepped into the church and nothing happened. I had expected something, a cry of protest from the church itself, or the ghosts of the long-dead patrons to come straight down from the rafters like avenging angels.

I looked around for another way out, or a weapon. There weren't even any Bibles to throw at him. "I did dream about you," I said, backing farther away.

"Of course you did. I know some of your clan have a smidgen of the sight."

"In my dreams you always died at the end. Every time."

He paused. A disconcerted look crossed his face. Then anger. "You are a clever little liar, aren't you?" His canine lips turned up in a smile. "You have only been on this earth for what, fifteen years? What's that to a thousand? A hundred thousand? We have been here forever. Since before your kind crawled its way up the slopes of Europe and put your vessels in the sea. What do you really know, child? Why should I honor a pact with such weaklings? Especially when you all taste so good." He crossed the floor and started up the aisle.

For every one of my steps, he took another, coming closer. And closer. His features were getting clearer: the slaver on his jaws, the anger in his eyes. But I could see his body was crisscrossed with deep scratch wounds from his battle with Gunnvor. And part of his left ear had been torn away. "It was my mother who died in the town square at Hvammstangi," he hissed. "She was over two thousand years old. Still so young. Killed by Thordy's father. I cannot even begin to describe the hate I have for your clan."

"We were only defending ourselves." I backed up a small set of stairs and bumped past the pulpit, an old ornate wood structure with a cross carved on the top. I was standing in the altar.

"You're prey, nothing more. You shouldn't fight back. When your parents come to collect your body, I will kill them, too. I won't stop until every last one of your clan has been removed from this world."

Skoll suddenly stopped just past the front row of pews. He tried to budge, but it was like his feet were set in glue. He struggled.

"You can't come in here," I said, sounding ten times more confident than I felt. My voice echoed through the church. "Your kind aren't allowed."

He snarled even louder, twisting and shaking. Then with a mighty effort he lifted a foot and planted it in the pulpit area. It began to smoke, then to burn. He raised his other foot. "I'm going to tear you to shreds."

A short pole with a cross on the top was leaning up against the wall. It was the kind a priest carried during a procession; it had perhaps been there for a hundred years.

Beside it was the large stained-glass window with an image of a lamb standing on a Bible, glowing white from the moon's light.

I grabbed the crucifix pole, held it in front of me. I felt a sudden rush of energy, like my ancestors were somehow lending me their strength. The pole vibrated like a lightning rod. I tightened my grip.

"That toy won't save you." Skoll grit his teeth and struggled forward, fixing me with his eyes. "I'll make you pay for every second of my pain."

The axe wound in his chest was bleeding anew, as if being inside the church had reopened it. The blood turned to smoke when it hit the floor. There *was* something magical about this place.

"You're bleeding," I said, enjoying the sight of him growing weaker. "Grandpa gets the last laugh."

He snarled and leapt. I swung the pole with all my might and a blinding flash burst across his flesh. He fell on his back with a scream.

Skoll jumped to his feet, rubbed at the burnt mass of hair on his chest. It fell away in clumps. He glared at me, a look of pure murderous intent. He leapt a second time, straight at me, and I struck him. The charge of energy nearly tore the pole from my arms. Skoll fell over, was up in the blink of an eye and after me again. This time I hit him square in the skull and the pole broke. An explosion of blinding white light surrounded us and he was blown back.

He landed in a crumpled heap, jerked about for a moment, then stopped. He looked dead; there were new gashes on his shoulder and forehead. He was shrinking back into his human form.

I dropped the shattered crucifix. My hands were black

and burning with pain. I could hardly open them.

Skoll lay across the steps, blocking my way out. I lifted my foot to step over him, felt him stir under me, then he grabbed my ankle and yanked me down.

36

"You little wretch," he yelled, throwing me against the wall. Even with his wounds and his power fading, he was so much stronger than I.

I used the windowsill to pull myself up and turned towards him. He was on his feet now, hunched over and clutching his ribs. One side of his face looked human, the other wolfish, as if he could no longer change into his full wolf form. He roared.

Everything slowed down. As he came at me, I reached into my coat pocket, grabbing the broken stub of wood that was still attached to the spearhead. Suddenly a new strength, like I had a direct line to Grettir himself, took hold of me. Skoll leapt and I set my feet, caught him below the chest with the spear, and pushed with all my might. He yelled and hurtled past, but as he did he reached out and snatched hold of my arm. I dropped the spearhead. His claws dug into my flesh as he dragged me along. He crashed through the stained-glass window, the image of the lamb smashing into a thousand pieces and showering us both. I was yanked around and my gut slammed into the windowsill. My arm felt like it had been pulled right out of its socket. I hung there, my head and chest over the edge, looking down, the blast of cold air bringing me to life.

Skoll dangled beneath me, his claws still biting into my arm. His other hand, half claws, half fingers, gripped the windowsill, leaving grooves in the wood. Below him was a drop into darkness off the edge of a cliff.

The church was cracking and groaning like he might pull the whole building over with him. His left hand slipped from the windowsill, caught my wrist, and he latched onto my arm with both hands.

I stared down into his face. It changed so that it looked more human. Not Uncle Thordy's face at all, but younger. His hair blonde and soft.

Andrew.

"You. Must. Help me." It sounded like Andrew's voice. His eyes were narrowed, his face helpless. "I can't hold on, sister. Don't let me fall," he said helplessly, "help me. Don't let me die again."

He looked so much like Andrew. So alive. So real.

"I've got you," I said, edging slightly ahead, trying to find a better grip with my feet. I started to pull him up. My brain was getting fuzzy. There was something about his eyes that wasn't right.

I pulled him an inch higher. Then another, so he could almost grab the windowsill on his own.

"You're a good sister. Higher."

He looked down. The back of his head was all black

curls and matted hair, his neck covered with fur. Not like Andrew at all.

I stopped pulling. He glanced back at me. Andrew's features were melting away like wax. Skoll's left hand shot up, grabbing at my hair.

"I don't want to be known as the girl who was killed by the wolf," I said and I struck him. Hard.

He snarled, changing back to his wolf form, trying to get a better grip, his muscles in his arm bunching together. I pummeled him again with a fist.

He swung away from the wall, taking a clump of my hair in his hand. He was hanging on only by his grip on my useless, dislocated arm.

Then, with one final effort, I pushed and he fell like a stone, down, down, down, screaming all the way. He hit the edge of the cliff wall, flipped around a couple of times, and finally crashed into the rocks below.

37

I stared out the window for what could have been an hour. Skoll was lying far below me with his arms spread, his body outlined by the moon. Flakes of snow drifted down, lightly covering him. In time I couldn't see him at all.

I leaned against the side of the church, breathing deeply, trying to gather my wits. I shook off the numbness, found the spearhead, and put it back in my pocket. The church was getting colder and colder and I needed to get home. I wandered out through the broken door and stumbled in the direction of Uncle Thordy's yard. I had to climb down a rock wall, careful not to put too much weight on my ankle. There were moments when I wanted to stop and just lie down, but a verse kept repeating itself over and over again in my head, in time with each step: *Cattle die, kinsmen die, I myself shall die, but there is one thing I know never dies: the reputation we leave behind at our death.*

I passed the alcove and Mordur was gone. So was Gunnvor's body. It was a lifetime before I neared the farm-yard. I was met by Michael and strangers in thick jackets. They looked like policemen. Two of them were carrying Mordur. The moment they got near I collapsed and they had to lift me. They wanted to know if I had seen Uncle Thordy. "He's dead, he's dead, he has to be," I whispered.

Then I passed out.

» 38 «

I awoke sweating from a fever. I was in a bed in a strange room. A shadow reached towards me and I froze, not able to move or yell out.

"It's okay, Angie," Sarah whispered, "it's just me." She dabbed my forehead with a cool facecloth, then put her hand on my cheek. A night-light shone dimly from the wall, casting her face in shadows. We were in our room at Uncle Thordy's house. "You're going to be okay."

My body wouldn't stop shaking. My joints felt like they were on fire. "I saw Grandpa. And Andrew."

I expected her to tell me I was crazy. "Good. That's so good. I feel better, knowing he was able to help us one more time."

"Where is Gunnvor? Did they find her body?"

Sarah looked at me. "No. No one found any body."

My brain tried to understand this. Maybe she'd gotten away. Wasn't dead. "Everything hurts," I whispered.

"You need another treatment. I'll get the others."

And before I could ask her who the others were, she was gone. She returned with a middle-aged man and two women. They seemed familiar. One of them looked so much like my mom it was uncanny.

"Who are you?" I asked. My teeth were chattering.

"Don't you remember?" Sarah said. "This is Uncle Thordy's brother and sisters. You met them the last time you woke up."

The last time? How long had I been out of it?

They circled me, spoke softly in Icelandic, and made me eat all this strange garlic-tasting stuff. They washed out my wounds with a liquid that stung ten times worse than iodine and smelled like stale beer. They didn't tell me what it was, and I didn't ask, but they hummed and whispered chants while they took care of me.

"You're going to the hospital now," Sarah explained, just before I slipped back into unconsciousness.

I woke up briefly on the trip to Hvammstangi. We were inside a large jeep, heading down the road. It was light out, but of course the sun was nowhere to be seen. I was leaning against Sarah; Michael sat beside me, clutching his arm. "Hi, Angie," he said, "back from the dead, I see."

I nodded. Turned my head. Mordur was laid out in the back, the woman who looked like my mom was holding him in place. "He's okay, isn't he?" I asked.

"Yes," Sarah said softly. "Yes, of course."

Then I was gone again. The next time I came to I was on a hospital bed and a doctor was bent over me, stitching my arm. It was frozen, of course. I watched a needle going in and out of the places where Skoll's claws had torn open my flesh, sealing them up. The doctor saw I was awake and explained he wasn't sure if my left arm would ever be the same. They would have to see after the swelling went down. I'd definitely have to go to a specialist back at home. My ankle was the only other major injury. All he could do was wrap it in a bandage and tell me not to go jogging.

I was given a room in the hospital and by the next day was feeling well enough to walk around. When Sarah and Michael visited me, Michael was sporting a cast from his wrist to his elbow. "Want to sign it? I've already got a great collection of Icelandic swear words."

I did sign, using my awkward right hand. I'd have to learn how to do a lot of things with that hand now.

"After everything thaws, they're going to hunt for Uncle Thordy's body," Sarah told me, "and then give him the funeral he deserves."

Would they find anything of Skoll? I wondered. Just thinking of him made my bones ache. I pushed him out of my mind.

"Oh, by the way," Sarah said, "Merry Christmas."

"What?"

"It's Christmas eve," Michael said, "but we're going to celebrate when our parents get here."

I was stunned. I must have slept through a full day. A short while later Sarah and Michael took me to Mordur's room and left me to sit with him. He was still unconscious, had not come to at all. I held his hand and spoke to him. I found myself telling him about what my house looked like back in North Dakota, where I went to school, what my favorite classes were, and what I was hoping to get for Christmas. It all just came pouring out of me. Finally, I told him how much I missed my Grandpa and my brother. I began to cry.

Still, he didn't wake up. Sarah told me they'd pulled a piece of what they thought was a claw from his neck, but it dissolved within seconds of being exposed to the air.

It was maybe the last little bit of Skoll left. The police only found ragged torn clothes where he had fallen. There was no other clue that he had ever existed. They searched Gunnvor's property, but both she and Onni were gone.

The next morning my parents arrived, along with Sarah and Michael's mom and dad, and we began preparing for Grandpa Thursten's funeral.

» 39 «

The funeral was held in a small Lutheran church in Hvammstangi. As we arrived, I knew it was a special occasion for the people of this area; there were a lot of townspeople standing outside. Inside, the church was packed with Icelanders dressed in black suits and dresses, waiting silently for us to arrive. I'd had no idea how important Grandpa Thursten had been to all the Icelanders here. A few friends had even flown all the way from Gimli. The front pews had been left empty for us, and we were guided to them by a young altar boy.

The minister who led the service said only a few words here and there; it was mostly songs sung one after another. I didn't know what they were about, though a few sounded familiar. There was something absolutely beautiful about the voices echoing in the rafters of the church, something that was, well, heavenly.

Near the end of the service, Uncle Robert, Michael and Sarah's dad, stood and spoke. He told the story of Grandpa Thursten's life, of his marriage, and of how there had been no one like him and that truly this was a sad day on earth, but a bright day in heaven for he would be reunited with his wife. He ended the eulogy by reading a passage from the myth about how the world reacted when the god Baldur died: *"All things wept. Fire wept. Steel wept. The mountains wept. The sky, the stones, the earth wept, the trees wept, all the animals wept for him."* By the time Uncle Robert was done, most everyone in the church wept too.

After the ceremony, they carried Grandpa's coffin out-doors and into a long hearse. It was late in the afternoon and the sun had slipped below the horizon, giving us only the slightest bit of light. I would never get used to the way the sun worked here. We stood by the hearse as people came up and hugged our parents or shook their hands. Then the mourners either walked home or got into their cars and drove away, leaving us to our grief.

It was a lot different than a funeral at home. Normally everyone would come to the gravesite. Maybe they did it differently here, just let the family look after their own. We climbed into our vehicles and followed the hearse out past Hvammstangi. We stopped along the edge of the ocean. My uncles and my mother carried Grandpa's coffin and set it on a boat piled high with kindling and smelling of gas. A fishing boat, the *Akraborg*, was waiting nearby in the water.

This wasn't a normal burial, my parents had explained to me. In fact, no one did this anymore, but it was what Grandpa had wanted. Then it dawned on me that this was why the people had gone on their way. Our business was ours alone. If no one from Hvammstangi saw it, then no one would have to report anything to the authorities.

My mother and Uncle Robert lit a torch and together walked through the snow to the side of the boat and touched an edge of the kindling. It burst into flames, circling Grandpa's coffin. The *Akraborg* pulled the funeral boat out onto the water, towards the horizon, then let it go. The flames grew higher and brighter and began to fade as the boat drifted into the distance.

We stood for a long time, watching. My mother and father held me between them and we wept.

Later, the family went to Uncle Thordy's and drank a lot of coffee, and people talked and sang and told stories about Grandpa, celebrating his life. Even we grandchildren threw in a few of the tall tales he had told us.

My mother gave me what Afi had left for me. It was a book he had carried with him his whole life, old and faded and written in Icelandic.

It was called *Grettir's Saga*.

» 40 «

The next few days were a blur of meeting other family members and seeing a little of the country. I hobbled around on my sore foot and took as many pictures as I could. There was never much light, so I was pretty sure only a handful would turn out. We did celebrate Christmas at a relative's home east of Hvammstangi. There was lots of food — most of it looked wonderful, some of it gross, but I couldn't really eat much.

On our last day, as I was laying out stuff to pack, Sarah burst into our room. "Mordur's awake," she said, "and he wants to see you."

My father drove me to town and dropped me off in front of the small hospital, saying he'd come back in a little while. I went straight to Mordur's room.

He was propped up in bed, dozing. When I sat down in the chair next to him, he slowly opened his eyes.

"Angie, I have a big hurt in my head."

I laughed. "I'm not surprised. You've been through the wringer."

"Tell me what happened."

I told him what I could remember, but I knew I'd left quite a few details out. "I'll give you the full story in a letter," I said. I handed him back his father's spearhead.

He took it from me and softly said, "Thanks. This means lots to me." He smiled. "My last real good memory is sitting by the fire, talking to you. You were going to speak all about yourself."

"I already did." I chuckled. He gave me a confused look. I explained that I had visited him while he was unconscious.

"I guess I was a good listener, I didn't interrupt you." He blinked. "You leave today, right?"

I nodded. "In a few hours."

"Thank you for letting me show you around. It was …" he struggled for words, "… it was an honor."

"No problem," I said, getting up. I felt tears in my eyes, but blinked them back. "We could have had a lot of fun. If everything had worked out differently." I leaned over him and kissed him on the lips. "Promise me you'll take care of yourself."

"As long as you promise to come back."

"I will."

» 41 «

Soon Iceland was far behind us and we were high in the air, the sun over one wingtip. Sarah was sitting beside me and Michael and our parents sat in front of us. The journey was quiet compared to our trip there, with Grandpa's long story about our great-grandfather.

"They never end happily, do they?" Sarah said. "The old Viking sagas. They're not like fairy tales; they don't end happily."

"No, they don't," I said. Then it struck me how one saga kept leading into the next. Story after story. "But Sarah," I said, raising an eyebrow, "when you think of it, the sagas never, ever really end."

» glossary «

Afi - Grandfather.

Bjúgnakrækir - A Christmas lad whose name means "sausage snatcher."

Bless - Good-bye.

Draugr - Ghost.

Fardu burt - Go away.

Flydu - Fly or flee.

Fellivetur - Slaughter winter.

Flatkökur - Hard bread charred without fat on a griddle.

Gluggagægir - A Christmas lad whose name means "window peeper."

Gódan dag - Good afternoon.

Góda nótt - Good night

Gott kvöld - Good evening.

Gravlax - Raw salmon cured in rock salt and dill.

Hangikjöt - Smoked lamb.

Hardfiskur - Cod, haddock, halibut, or catfish that has been beaten and hung up to dry on racks.

Huldu Folk - The "hidden people," little elf-like people of Icelandic folklore.

Jólasveinar - Yuletide/Christmas lads. Thirteen imps in the Icelandic Christmas tradition who visit, one a day, for thirteen days before Christmas Eve. They leave little presents for the children in shoes that have been put on the windowsill the night before. If the children have been naughty, the imps leave a potato or a reminder that good behavior is better.

Logga - Slang, shortened version of *logreglumadur*, which means police officer.

Loup-garou - Werewolf (French).

Lupinus - Wolf (Latin).

Niflheim – A realm of freezing mist and darkness. *Hel*, the realm of the dead, lies within it.

Nordurleid - A bus line whose name means "North Way" or "North Route."

Pottasleikir - A Christmas lad whose name means "pot licker."

Ragnarok - The final battle between the gods and the giants in Old Norse mythology.

Skyr - A butter-like spread made from milk and sour cream. Icelanders eat *skyr* as a dessert with sugar or cream or fruit.

Stúfur - A Christmas lad whose name means "itty bitty."

Svid - Singed sheep's head, sawn in two, boiled, and eaten fresh, pickled, or jellied.

Úlfr-madr - Wolf man.

Úlfslikid - Wolf thing.

Uppvakníngur - A spirit that has been awakened from the dead. Zombie.

author's note

The question I am most often asked about the Northern Frights series is: "Where did you get your ideas?" It's a common question from teachers, students, and other readers. The ideas for the stories about Sarah, Michael, and Angie came from some wonderful, inspirational Icelandic sagas and Old Norse myths. There are far too many to list, but I thought I'd mention a few of the most influential collections:

Myths of the Norsemen by Roger Lancelyn Green, published by Penguin Books. This is a fairly easy read with illustrations. There's a good selection of myths and folktales, including Sigurd's epic battle with Fafnir the dragon.

The Norse Myths by Kevin Crossley-Holland, published by Penguin Books. This is one of the most eloquent adaptations of the Norse myths about Loki, Thor, Odin, and all the other gods. It's full of poetic language and extensive notes on the text. A warning though, it is also true to the bawdy nature of the original myths.

Grettir's Saga translated by Denton Fox and Hermann Pálsson, published by University of Toronto Press. This would be tough slogging for younger readers, but you librarian and adult readers (I know you're out there) might be interested in reading this account of Grettir the Strong's life.

For anyone who wants to know more about Iceland, just visit http://www.samkoma.com. Samkoma means "meeting place," and at this site you can search for any topic under the Icelandic sun.

And finally, if you have any comments or want to know more about the Northern Frights series, or about me, just drop by http://www.arthurslade.com.

Bless,
Art

More books in the Northern Frights series:

Draugr
(Arthur G. Slade)

Grandpa was going to murder us. Not with an axe. Not with a shovel. But with words.

When Sarah, Michael, and Angie arrive from the US to spend summer vacation with their grandpa in Gimli, Manitoba, they are prepared for his scary stories based on Icelandic mythology. But they are anything but prepared when events from the story about a *draugr* – a man who comes back from the dead — begin to happen to them.

A fascinating, well-told story. Highly recommended. – KLIATT

… characters are well-drawn … stands above much of its competition in writing and plot development. – *Quill & Quire*

… definitely a higher class example of the horror genre … fascinating! – *Canadian Materials*

1-55143-094-0; $7.95 CAN, $6.95 USA

The Haunting of Drang Island
(Arthur G. Slade)

If you're going to die, die with your boots on. That's what my Grandpa Thursten used to say.

When Michael and his father arrive on Drang Island for a camping trip, they find that all the rumors they've heard are true. The island is desolate, sparsely populated, and far from civilization. It seems the perfect place for Michael's father to finish the last chapters of his book of Norse stories.

Unfortunately it soon becomes apparent that some of the other rumors they've heard about Drang Island — stories about spirits, strange sacrifices, and a serpent lurking in the ocean — might also be true!

The scare is the thing here and this book won't disappoint.
      — School Library Journal

… Slade has tapped into a fascinating area …
      — Resource Links

1-55143-111-4; $7.95 CAN, $6.95 USA